DOCTOR'S EMERGENCY FIANCÉE

KATE MACGUIRE

MEDICAL ROMANCE

Recycling programs for this product may not exist in your area

ISBN-13: 978-1-335-95289-9

Doctor's Emergency Fiancée

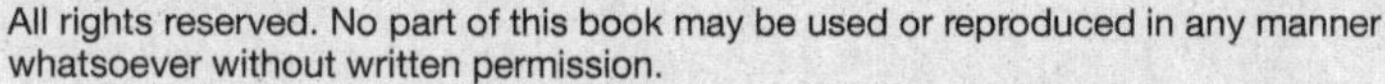

For questions and comments about the quality of this book, please contact us at CustomerService@Harlequin.com.

Harlequin Enterprises ULC
22 Adelaide St. West, 41st Floor
Toronto, Ontario M5H 4E3, Canada
www.Harlequin.com

HarperCollins Publishers
Macken House, 39/40 Mayor Street Upper
Dublin 1, D01 C9W8, Ireland
www.HarperCollins.com

Printed in U.S.A.

1 2 3 4 5 6 7 8 9 10 HDC 29 28 27 26

“You sly fox,” Jess said, setting the flowers back on his desk, then dropping back into the chair. “Start talking, mister.”

God, that man hated to talk. It was obvious from the rigid set of Nolan’s shoulders and how his fingers fidgeted at his cuffs. He’d probably be more enthusiastic if she just asked him to defuse a bomb with his stethoscope.

He coughed discreetly. “As I said, the wedding will be hosted at my family’s vineyard in Napa Valley. I am told many people enjoy Napa Valley for weekend excursions. If you are one of such people, I would, of course, cover all of your expenses for the weekend.”

“But I have to be your fiancée?”

His jaw was so tight, it practically quivered. “Ideally, yes.”

Jess felt her body warm with delight. The heat settled in her chest and spiraled down her spine as she watched Nolan fidget and squirm. Every tiny movement screamed of his discomfort. She felt like a cat who had cornered her prey, and she wanted to draw out the delicious torture as long as possible.

Dear Reader,

Welcome to the wonderfully chaotic world of Jess and Nolan! If you love mismatched personalities, stubborn hearts and living in a world of rules that were meant to be broken, this story is for you.

Nolan is a stickler-for-rules pediatrician who meets his match in the bright, unstoppable force of Jessica Hayes. His clipped orders versus her spontaneous charm, his spreadsheets versus her musings, and the very awkward—yet irresistible—fake engagement that forces them to see beyond the chaos and into the possibility of true love and understanding.

So grab your coffee and fluffy socks—time to enjoy the ride! Emergency rescues, vending machine mishaps and heart-fluttering sparring sessions await.

Happy reading!

Kate MacGuire

katemacguire.com

@KateWritesRomance

Kate MacGuire has loved writing since forever, which led to a career in journalism and public relations. Her short fiction won the Swarthout Award and placed third in the 2020 Women's National Book Association writing contest. Medical romance has always been her guilty pleasure, so she is thrilled to be writing novels for Harlequin's Medical Romance line. When she's not pounding away on the keyboard, Kate co-runs Camp Runamuk with her husband, keeping its two unruly campers in line in the beautiful woodlands of North Carolina. Visit katemacguire.com for updates and stories.

Books by Kate MacGuire

Harlequin Medical Romance

Resisting the Off-Limits Pediatrician
City Doc for the Single Mom
Bump in Their Italian Fling

Visit the Author Profile page at Harlequin.com.

In Memory of Sheila Hodgson,
Senior Editor of Harlequin Medical Romance

Just one collaboration with you
gave me a lifetime of lessons. Thank you.

CHAPTER ONE

THE HORIZON BAY MEDICAL INSTITUTE was a massive L-shaped health campus, built atop former railyards that had brought the steel and labor needed to transform an old Catholic mission into the major port city of San Francisco. From the outside, the clean, deliberate lines of the hospital didn't whisper of history. Its openness and space announced the future—bright, clinical, and full of quiet urgency.

Dr. Jessica Hayes navigated her SUV down the wide hospital driveway, sidewalks and young trees flanking her on both sides. The hospital's landscaping architect had done an admirable job of softening the facility's sharp angles and long lines with bands of greenery that spilled from terraces and rooftop gardens. In the distance, she could hear the clang of construction and shouted orders as a road improvement crew shut down their worksite for the day.

Jess dashed through the sliding doors of the hospital with two minutes to spare before her shift started. The moist fog of San Francisco's night air had left her hair more unmanageable than usual, but there was no time to primp in the locker room. She pulled it into a messy ponytail, draped her stethoscope around her neck, and swiped into the electronic records system.

While the software downloaded the files, she scanned the patient tracking board. There were several patients waiting, a few labs pending, and only one bright red critical alert. That was unusually quiet for the busy hospital she had called home for the past year.

Lena, the charge nurse on duty, joined her at the workstation. "Been a dink night so far." She crossed her fingers. "Let's hope it holds."

"Well, now it won't!" Jess laughed. "You just jinxed it!" A dink night was when the emergency department was filled with mostly nonserious cases. Patients with little "dinks" instead of the usual parade of trauma and life-or-death cases. It would be nice to have a low-pressure night, but Jess wasn't going to hold her breath. Things could change on a dime around here.

She scanned the PEM column on the tracking board, where pediatric cases were coded. As an emergency medicine doctor, Jess could handle any case that came through the department. But her fellowship in pediatrics would make her the priority choice for most of the pediatric cases.

Jess considered her choices. There was a five-year-old who couldn't stop hiccuping, a teen who burned herself trying a cooking hack she saw on social media, and a four-year-old with a laceration to the forehead. Kids sure could get themselves into big trouble.

"I'll take the four-year-old lac." She grabbed a computer tablet, then clipped some of the new animals she bought at the dollar store to her stethoscope. Distractions were king when working with toddlers.

Jess slipped into the trauma bay and found a mother sitting on a chair, a little boy on her lap. The woman was clearly distressed—her lashes wet with tears as she pressed a white towel to the boy's forehead. But the boy was calm as could be. His wavy hair had fallen forward as he focused on his mother's cell phone, playing some kind of game with lots of cartoon music and digital giggles.

Jess gave the mother a reassuring smile, then greeted the boy. "Hi, Brian! My name is Dr. Hayes. I heard you got an owie today?"

Brian glanced her way, then back to the phone. A sudden burst of silly music had captured his attention.

"Oh, I feel just awful," the woman said, clutching the boy tighter. "He was brushing his teeth and I left the bathroom for *one second*! Just to find his pajamas. That's when he tumbled off the step stool and hit his head on the counter."

Classic toddler-meets-gravity situation. Jess

mentally crossed her fingers as Lena had, hoping this might be another dink case.

Jess began taking notes. "Did he lose consciousness after the fall?"

"No. He just cried a little."

"Did he feel sick to his stomach or have any behavior changes?"

Though the woman said no, she still seemed on the verge of tears.

Jess refocused on Brian. "Can I see your owie, friend?"

He nodded once, solemnly. Jess slowly peeled the towel away from Brian's forehead, hoping the towel's fibers had not embedded in the cut.

But the towel was perfectly white. Jess's gaze scanned the boy's forehead up and down, and side to side. What was she missing? There was nothing to see but the smooth, unblemished forehead of an adorable toddler.

The mother pressed her fingers to her mouth. "Do you think the stitches will leave a scar?" she asked, her voice shaky and frail.

Jess was mystified. Could the laceration be higher than she thought? She gently parted the boy's hair, looking for an injury in the scalp. But she found nothing.

"I'm sorry. Can you show me where Brian's injury is?"

The mother leaned forward, then pointed at a spot in his hairline. Jess peered closer and then she saw it. The tiniest scratch in the history of scratches. Not even deep enough to produce a single drop of blood.

Lena was right. This was going to be a dink night.

"I feel awful, just awful! My boy is going to be scarred for life and it's my fault!" A single tear traced her cheek.

Jess considered her options. Most doctors in her situation would be plenty irritated with this mother by now. Emergency departments needed to be available for the worst of the worst cases, not clogged up with nonurgent ones. A mother like this could be accused of being a drama queen, or worse, using her son's health to garner attention for herself.

Jess took in the woman's smooth skin and bright eyes. Her gut told her this mother wasn't trying to abuse the hospital's emergency department. She appeared to be a new mom, and a young one at that. Two years ago, she might have been hanging out with her friends, trying new mascara, and downloading the latest music from her favorite bands. Now she was charged with keeping this small, defenseless human being alive and in good health, no matter what kind of trouble he got himself in.

So no, she wasn't going to give this young mother a lecture about contacting her pediatrician's triage nurse for injuries like this. That would only make her feel foolish and perhaps lead her to second-guess her judgment in the future. Anyone could make a mistake. She didn't need to make a big deal about it, especially on a night like this.

Jess flashed Brian's mom her best smile. "Oh no, I don't think we have to worry about surgery or scars tonight. We'll just get Brian fixed up here, then you can go home."

The mother's shoulders dropped a little, but the little wrinkle between her brows remained. Jess knew that technically, she should send Brian and mom on their way. But it was still quiet in the ED, and Lena would page her if she was needed elsewhere.

So, she made a show of laying out long swabs, ointment, and a Band-Aid. Then let Brian choose one of her stethoscope buddies (a koala) to play with while she treated his "wound." Brian seemed to enjoy the attention, finally abandoning the phone so he could answer all of Jess's questions about pets, school, and favorite games.

"There! All better." She helped the boy off the table, fully expecting his mom to be happy and relieved. But that little wrinkle remained.

"Do you think he needs a consultation with a dermatologist? You know, to prevent a scar?"

"I'm sorry, but we don't have a dermatologist on staff at night." Before she could reassure the mother that a consultation probably wasn't necessary, Lena jumped into the chat.

"But we have a pediatrician on call. Dr. Stone."

Jess felt her shoulders stiffen and heart plummet to her shoes. Why on earth had Lena even suggested a consult with Dr. Nolan Stone? Everyone knew she and Nolan did not see eye to eye on…just about everything. He was all data and protocols and best standards of care. Stiff upper lip and toe the line and all that jazz. While she believed data and protocols were a good starting point, it was just as important to see the big picture too. Sometimes rules needed to be flexed a little to provide the best patient care.

"Could we speak to him?" the mother asked. "I would just appreciate a second opinion."

Oh, you'll get that and so much more, Jess thought as she held her smile, her cheeks tight with the effort. "You sure there's no one else around?" she asked Lena through clenched teeth.

"Nope!" Lena responded before flipping the curtain aside to make her escape. But not before Jess caught a glimpse of the smile that was making her mouth dance. That only confirmed her long-running suspicion that some of the staff enjoyed her clashes with Nolan and saw them as a welcome distraction during long night shifts.

After double and triple checking that the mother wouldn't prefer to follow up with her pediatrician, Jess reluctantly sent a page through the electronic medical records system. Dr. Stone responded almost immediately, letting her know that he was dealing with a rash of food poisoning cases from a boys' basketball camp. That was fine by her. She was in no hurry to listen to the long, dry lecture that Nolan was sure to deliver.

Jess headed to the break room, her stomach growling. She had stayed late at her father's rehab center, where he was recovering from a hip fracture he had sustained at their family farm in Minnesota. She had stayed late, trying in vain to get him to eat a little more dinner or leave his room for a stroll around the center's garden. She'd had no time to eat before her night shift, and there was no way she could face Nolan on an empty stomach. Being paged for a nonexistent wound was going to annoy him to no end. And when Jess tried to explain this was about calming a nervous mother, he wouldn't get that at all. She could almost hear the precision in his clipped speech as he outlined the proper patient care protocols for her…again.

She shouldn't take it personally—Nolan had a reputation for treating everyone like a student doctor in training. But she seemed to be the only doctor annoyed by his rigid methods. Her female colleagues had leaned into his controlling tendencies, calling him "The Professor" when he wasn't around and exchanging sly winks as they made suggestive jokes about after-hours "lessons."

Jess didn't get the appeal. Okay, the man was *somewhat* attractive…if you were stranded on a desert island with nothing to do for forty years.

But his fussy, judgmental vibe did not work for her at all. "Professor" is not what she would call him. More like a guard dog with a bone. Once he set his mind to a certain outcome, he wasn't going to let go until *he* was satisfied.

A leftover ham sandwich awaited her in the staff refrigerator. As she headed towards it, she was busy practicing her responses to Nolan's expected questions when she picked up a snippet of a conversation going on in the break room. She heard the unmistakable syllables of Evan's name, then hers, followed by *well, you know...*

Jess paused in the hallway, biting her lip as she felt heat race to her cheeks. She could turn on her heel if she wanted. Go back to her workspace and no one in that break room would ever be the wiser. If she just ignored the gossip and innuendo, things would eventually die down. Or so she told herself, even though the chatter had shown few signs of abating despite the truth coming out three months ago.

She and Evan's short *relationship*—if you could call it that—was long over. But she knew that her co-workers didn't call it a relationship. They called it an affair, and they still held it against Jess. Because Evan—popular, sunny, charismatic Evan—was a married man when he dated Jess, a detail he had neglected to share with her.

Were it not for the hospital's Fun in the Sun summer fundraiser, Jess might never have discovered the truth. She had volunteered to run the auction, making sure that everyone received the raffle tickets they had purchased.

What a shock it had been, seeing "Dr. Evan Sims & Mrs. Sienna Sims" included in the list. Jess felt the air whoosh out of her as she tried to make sense of what she was seeing. Her brain just refused to put two and two together; her denial was just too strong.

So, she had gone to his office, list in hand and demanded an explanation. *It's complicated*, he said. Complicated meaning he wasn't separated or divorced. Just "considering his options."

The next three months of her life were a blur of shame, guilt, and going emotionally numb so she could function at work. When Evan took a job out of state, it made her professional life nominally easier. No more worrying about running into him in the cafeteria or around the hospital.

But it had also left her alone to face the fallout of their brief fling. Like what was waiting for her in the break room. Jess took a deep breath to brace herself, then turned the corner into the break room. The conversation came to a sudden halt, as she had known it would. No one said a word as she rooted in the refrigerator, looking in vain for the container she had labeled with her name in big block letters. But it was nowhere to be found, either taken or tossed between her shifts.

To save face, she grabbed a bottle of water provided by the hospital and smiled at the small group of nurses. They sat frozen, staring down at the table, probably wondering if she had overheard their chatter. Hopefully the gossip would end soon, so she could be Just Jess again and not feel like she had a scarlet letter pinned to her chest for the rest of her career.

Jess beat a quick retreat to her workspace, her stomach growling with every step. Food would have to wait until she had time to dash to the cafeteria during her dinner break in a few hours.

She dropped into a chair at a staff workstation to write up her notes on Brian. But first she pressed her cool hands to her warm cheeks, willing herself to calm down. These moments of gossip never failed to fill her with shame. She felt so gullible, so foolish—falling for every excuse Evan had given to explain his lack of availability, his long and unexplained absences. She had thought she was being an understanding girlfriend when, in fact, she had been a fool.

Sometimes she was tempted to share the truth with a colleague. But it felt hopeless. Evan had been adored by the hospital staff. He had one of those chameleon personalities, which could charm his way out of any trouble. While she had a reputation for being spirited to the point of impulsive, willing to flex rules on occasion. It wasn't a huge jump for colleagues to believe that Evan had been a disaster of her own making. Sometimes she thought they were right.

She shook her head to clear her thoughts. Enough of that nonsense—it was time to focus on work. That and keeping tabs on her dad as he recovered from pneumonia had kept her busy enough since Evan had left Horizon Bay.

Jess's stomach growled hard, letting her know she could no longer ignore her hunger. Her only option was Vendora, the jerk of a vending machine down the hall near the elevators. Its only redeeming quality was carrying her favorite brand of corn chips. Otherwise, it was a thieving bandit that loved to steal and torture her to no end.

Just one bag of her favorite corn chips left. Man, she was *not* in the mood to be messed with. She splayed her hand against the glass. "All right, Vendora. You want to do this the easy way…or the hard way? It's up to you."

Her vending nemesis didn't respond, but Jess felt sure it knew she meant business. She swiped her card, then pressed J1, feeling like she was at a roulette table in Vegas. The spiral coil came to life with a whirring sound, pushing the corn chips her way inch by tantalizing inch.

Just when Jess thought it was going to be a good night, the coil stopped whirring. The tantalizing yellow and orange bag of chips dangled just out of reach. Its gentle shimmy felt like a taunt.

Jess felt her mouth salivate while another warm

flush rushed to her cheeks. This night was starting to get on her nerves. First the gossip, then her stolen sandwich, now this?

"No!" she muttered, smacking the glass with her hand. This damn machine was so moody. Sometimes it delivered the chips, other times it stopped short. Once it gave her two bags of chips for no reason at all.

Vendora was impervious to her abuse. If she swiped her card again, she'd get the chips for sure. But the unfairness of it irked her. Especially because she knew there was another way.

She glanced over both shoulders. The coast was clear. "Last chance, Vendora. Give up those chips or this is gonna get real personal."

The vending machine stood stoic and stubborn.

"Fine. You've made your choice." Jess looked around one more time before kneeling in front of the machine. If she got herself in just the right position, she could snake her arm past the chute flap. She just had to press her shoulder way down and her butt way up, then wiggle her fingers against the chips to free them from the delivery arm. *Easy peasy lemon squeezy.*

Jess dropped her upper body so she could press her shoulder against the machine. Her arm snaked past the delivery flap, and she felt her fingers brush against her prize.

She was almost there.

Just a tiny bit further...

* * *

Nolan sat at his immaculately organized desk, every pen, paper, and file perfectly aligned to the sharp angles of his desk. The glow of his computer screen reflected off the polished mahogany as he stared at his computer screen, a headache flirting with his furrowed brow.

Dear Mother and Father,
I regret to inform you...

No, no—that was far too formal. They would think he was about to deliver a devastating diagnosis instead of a little bad news. He backspaced with deliberate, clipped keystrokes until the screen was blank.

Nolan steepled his fingers under his chin as he contemplated the best approach. A window smudge caught his attention. He walked over for a closer look, then retrieved the glass cleaner and a soft rag from a cabinet. He sprayed and polished the window, examined the glass again, then returned the cleaning supplies before heading back to his desk.

If only his current project was as easy to tidy up.

Dear Mom and Dad, I'm sorry to say that...

His fingers hovered over the keyboard, unsure what to write next. Who has ever typed the words *I am sorry I will not be bringing my imaginary fiancée to Connor's wedding?* No one ever was his best guess, but nevertheless, here he was.

His fingers dropped back onto the keyboard. Mercifully, his phone rang.

"We've got a problem with the insurance company for the Jasper boy." Lena, ever efficient and focused, delivered the message without fanfare.

"Is that the boy with the broken arm?"

"Yep. They're denying coverage, saying we are an out-of-network hospital. His family either pays out of pocket, or he must travel across town to an approved facility."

Nolan mentally rehashed the case. He had seen the boy earlier that day—an eight-year-old with a badly fractured arm that would need surgery to stabilize the shattered fragments that could injure his nerves or blood vessels. Nolan knew Horizon Bay was out-of-network, but he had thoroughly reviewed the plan's exception policies and had *extensively* documented the circumstances that warranted an exception being made in this case.

Had the insurance reviewer even read his documentation? Damn, it annoyed him when people didn't read his notes.

Nolan could hear a commotion in the background. Lena undoubtedly had better things to do than bicker with insurance reviewers.

"Patch them through," he told her. "I'll take care of it."

His phone rang a few seconds later.

"Good evening, Dr. Stone. I am Dr. Brennan, medical reviewer for Western Health. Based on the information provided, this case does not meet our criteria for emergent surgical intervention at an out-of-network facility. You may proceed with transfer to the approved facility listed in your electronic portal."

There was no doubt Dr. Brennan was reading from a well-worn script. Nolan's grip tightened on the phone. He took a deep breath and pushed down his annoyance. Feelings were only going to muck things up during this phone call. If he wanted to win this battle, he needed to ignore his feelings and focus on the evidence.

"My patient isn't being transferred anywhere until he's truly stabilized. I'm sure you're familiar with EMTALA? That's *federal* law and it requires that a comminuted pediatric forearm fracture with neurovascular risk be stabilized surgically."

"Our policy classifies splinting as sufficient…"

"Your policy does not supersede federal law, Dr. Brennan. Furthermore, I have reviewed Western Health's policy. *Your* plan mandates exceptions when a delay in care could cause measurable harm. If you had reviewed my notes, you would see that a transfer risks displacement, nerve injury, and compartment syndrome."

"I have reviewed your notes, Dr. Stone, and will restate our position. The risk is minimal if the arm is immobilized."

"Wrong again. Check the documentation. Finally, has Western Health considered its own liabilities in this matter? If the child loses nerve function due to unnecessary transport, this would be considered a preventable injury. That's legally actionable, Dr. Brennan."

There was a long pause on the reviewer's end. Then, "One moment, Dr. Stone, while I consult my supervisor."

"You do that."

Nolan said stiff and rigid, drumming his fingers against the desk. These insurance battles were tiresome, but Nolan had learned how to play the game. He just needed to know the data better than anyone else. Just more proof that success in life was earned, even when it came to caring for his patients.

After several minutes of loopy elevator music, the reviewer returned to the line. "Authorization has been approved. You may proceed with surgery at your facility. The approval number is..."

Nolan unscrewed his fountain pen and recorded the number with neat, uniform strokes.

Damn straight, he wanted to crow. *'Bout time you guys finally read your own policies*. But he kept those thoughts to himself.

"I appreciate your diligence," he said, then hung up, feeling triumphant to have won yet another battle on his patients' behalf.

But those good feelings were soon overshadowed by the task at hand. He still didn't know what to tell his parents. They, especially his mother, were going to be so disappointed that he wouldn't have a plus-one for Connor's wedding. Her excitement at the prospect of him getting married had been palatable, even across the wide state of California.

Blurting was hardly his modus operandi, but when his mother began musing which of his ex-girlfriends might be divorced by now, and therefore *datable*, he knew he had to put a hard stop to that.

Nolan didn't want to run into any ex anywhere. Nor did he want to rehash the tiresome subject of his love life…or lack of one. So, he just said he didn't need a date. She had pressed for more details while his pager was ringing like a five-alarm fire, and his blood sugar was crashing from lack of food. It was stupid—he knew that now—but he had impulsively decided to go the cryptic route.

Who knows, Mom, maybe you'll be planning two weddings this year.

She was supposed to laugh! Why on earth would she believe he had a fiancée? He never dated—at least not seriously—and hadn't brought a woman home for the family to meet since high school. Between his shifts as a pediatric hospitalist, his publication work, and the frequent invitations to speak at pediatric conferences, there was little time for him to date, let alone get engaged.

So, he never expected her to take him at face value. But she did and the next thing he knew, he was being peppered with text messages congratulating him on his engagement and wanting to know all about his "fiancée."

He should have corrected the matter immediately. It would have been so much easier! Instead, he had relied on his brother's poor nuptial record for escape. Connor had been engaged four times before this wedding. It wasn't exactly illogical to think that his little problem would take care of itself. All he had to do was wait for Connor to announce the wedding was off, then he could claim things didn't work out with his "fiancée" and life would get back to normal.

But with the wedding less than a month away, Nolan's hopes for an easy escape were fading. His mother called him every day—often multiple times a day. *What is she like? Where did you meet? Should I rearrange the guest room so she can stay longer?*

Why had he let it go this far? Why had he even promised a fiancée in the first place? Was it possible he was still competing with Connor for their father's attention…and love?

He would like to believe that he was past that now. He had made peace with the fact that he was never going to have that easygoing camaraderie that Connor shared with their father. They were both cut from the same cloth: gifted athletes who had found their fame and fortune in professional football. Where Nolan had been built more like his mother, reticent and cerebral.

Those traits had made him feel like an alien to his father. He was someone his father loved but didn't understand. But when his academic gifts allowed him to start college at age fourteen, his father took note of him—in a big way. This, Nolan learned, was *his* path to his father's heart: hard work, lots of sacrifice, and the success that came with it.

But now he was in uncharted territory. His brother was getting married, for real this time. Was Nolan feeling inadequate because of Connor's wedding? Was producing a fake fiancée his way of keeping up…again?

He didn't know for sure. But he did know he had put his mother off for as long as he could, hiding behind work and voicemail and his own paralyzing guilt. He felt terrible he had let it go this far. It was time to get things straightened out before the farce got any more complicated.

Dear Mom and Dad,
There is no easy way to say this. I'm afraid we have a bit of a misunderstanding. I will not be bringing…

His computer dinged, indicating a notification from the EMR system. Nolan braced himself for another fight with the insurance company. But no, this was much worse. Dr. Jessica Hayes was requesting a pediatric consult.

Nolan closed his eyes and leaned back against his chair. He tried to push down the flurry of emotions that he felt whenever Dr. Hayes was in his orbit.

Why did she drive him so crazy? It wasn't a question of skill; she was a very talented doctor for sure. More than that, patients loved her. Even the hospital administrators loved her. Everywhere she went, she left a veritable trail of sparkly rainbows and unicorns in her wake.

So, why did she get under his skin so much? For starters, she was tiny—so tiny that every time he got annoyed, he felt like a grumpy giant scolding a defenseless waif.

Second, she possessed a wicked smile. It was her secret weapon, no doubt. It hit him like a Vegas casino sign, flashing so bright he couldn't look away. Endlessly distracting. And he hated distractions.

But worst of all was her constant second-guessing. *But Dr Stone, don't you think…*and *maybe if the patient felt more heard...*

She loaded every decision with feelings and possibilities. It made him feel like a drill sergeant discussing philosophy on the battlefield.

Medicine was science, dammit! And the rules were perfectly clear. Know the protocols, stick to well-defined standards and all would end well.

Why Dr. Hayes wanted to muddy the waters was beyond him. Even more mysterious was how Miss-Sunshine-and-Moonbeams had wound up in the emergency department, a place that could be full of trauma and despair.

Curiosity had gotten the better of him, and he had once asked her if she wouldn't be happier working in pediatrics. It was easy to imagine her at a family clinic where she could entertain toddlers with her endless supply of cheerful optimism and collection of weird animals she clipped to her stethoscope, far from the horrors of emergency medicine.

She had just gifted him a sweet, retina-searing smile. "Well, Dr. Stone, imagine being rushed to the emergency department on the worst day of your life. Which would you prefer—a doctor who thought your chances were kind of *meh*, or one who fiercely believed in *you*?"

He still didn't know what the hell that meant. It only reinforced his commitment to keeping his interactions with Dr. Hayes to a bare minimum.

Still, consulting with Dr. Hayes was minutely less torturous than sparring with insurance medical reviewers. He headed to the elevator and braced himself for the glittersplosion that would soon be blasted his way.

Exiting the elevator, he needed to veer left into the emergency department. But something in his peripheral vision caught his attention. It was a strange blob of pink and white near the vending machine. He couldn't make sense of its shape and form until it wiggled and cursed.

It appeared to be a person. On the floor, in a strange position. Wearing fuchsia pink scrubs, liberally sprinkled with little white bunnies. A stethoscope lay coiled on the floor, its animal collection confirming his suspicions.

There was only one person this could be. Jess's back was to Nolan, completely oblivious to his presence, half pressed against the vending machine like she was trying to dance with it. She had one arm shoved up inside the slot, tugging at a bag of chips that refused to budge.

Nolan slowly approached, his hands stuffed in his pockets. Somehow, this was shaping up to be even stranger than their usual interactions.

He stopped and rocked back on his heels. "Dr. Hayes?"

The pink-and-white rabbit figure jumped a little. "Yes?"

"I believe you requested a consult."

Her head slumped. "I did."

"Would you like to do that now?"

Her sigh was audible. "Male patient, four years old, reported head laceration. I…uh…checked the wound—just a small scratch…"

"Dr. Hayes?"

"Yes?"

"Would you care to extricate yourself from the vending machine first?"

Jess wiggled her arm vigorously, then stopped. "No, Dr. Stone. I would not."

The headache that had been brewing earlier was coming into its full power. Nolan pinched the bridge of his nose. "Continue."

"The mother was agitated and requested a consult, so…here we are."

"So, what exactly are we consulting about?"

"The four-year-old with a laceration to his forehead."

"The *nonexistent* laceration, correct?"

"That's correct."

Nolan practically threw up his hands. "So, why are we here?"

"The mother was quite nervous and feeling guilty. It was a slow night in the ED, so I saw no harm in honoring her request for a consult."

Nolan's eyes narrowed as he took in the scene, part disbelief, part irritation. "Dr. Hayes," he said, voice tight with controlled exasperation, "best practices don't exactly support consulting peds for a four-year-old with a superficial scratch just because the parent is anxious. We triage based on medical necessity, not maternal nerves. Now, if we're done here…"

But apparently he wasn't done, because he couldn't stop his gaze from lingering despite himself. Noticing her compromised angle against the vending machine, the maddeningly distracting curve of her backside.

"That is to say," he added, his jaw so tight he feared a cracked tooth. "Perhaps you could dedicate yourself a bit more selectively."

He had turned and taken a step toward the elevator when she answered. "Perhaps you could learn to go with the flow, sir."

He turned back. "Sorry?"

She shook her arm vigorously again, then gave up. He saw the problem now. She had caught the edge of her long-sleeved crew shirt on the metal vending arm. Despite her best efforts, the vending machine was not going to let her go. It had her pinned so she couldn't escape and couldn't even face him for a proper sparring session.

But that didn't stop her from trying. "I'm just saying that most of the other pediatricians get it. Some families require more care and feeding than others. This mother needed a little more from us. So, why can't you cut her a break?"

He disliked her pink bunny scrubs almost as much as he disliked being interrupted from his work for no good reason. But Jess had been brave to honor that mother's request, knowing full well how he'd respond. Braver still to tell him he was being a jerk, which he was.

Nolan contemplated the best way to find those words for her.

"You appear to be having some technical trouble. Shall I call maintenance?"

She glanced over her shoulder as best she could in her compromised position. There was perhaps a slight curve to her mouth.

"Very kind of you, Dr. Stone. But I'm good."

He couldn't imagine how. But it was high time he took his leave, before their interaction got any stranger.

CHAPTER TWO

JESSICA FINALLY WRENCHED herself free from the vending machine, ripping her sleeve in the process. Damn it—that was her favorite shirt. She awkwardly pulled herself up, brushing at the dirt that smudged her arms and knees. What an embarrassing fiasco. And she never even got the damn bag of chips.

Note to self, she muttered on her way back to the emergency department. *Stock your own supply of corn chips...by the case!*

She slinked back to the emergency department, hot with humiliation. Of all the people who could have found her embedded in the vending machine, why did it have to be The Professor? More to the point, why couldn't that guy ever lighten up?

She spent the rest of her shift burying herself in work. No breaks, no chitchat, no thinking. Staying busy was the key to staying out of trouble. It reminded her of some folksy phrase she had heard long ago, maybe from her mother. But it was hard to know for sure—her mother had died when she was so young.

She signed off on her last case for the night. Just past the hospital doors, the sun was lightening the navy blue sky. She could see pale gold bleeding into the soft pinks of the city's rooftops. The fresh new day merged with the chaos of the night—beeping monitors, wailing kids, freshly brewed coffee, and antiseptic. All woven together into the fabric of her life.

She had just passed the nursing station on her way out when someone called her name.

"Those are for you," a young nurse said, indicating a huge bouquet of flowers on the counter. It was impossibly tall and bursting with fuchsia peonies and deep purple orchids. Silk ribbons cascaded down the vase, matching the riot of colorful blooms.

For one paralyzing moment, Jess thought they might be from Evan. Was it possible he was sending her flowers to apologize for the impossible situation he had left her in? For lying to her? For compromising her values without her permission?

The anger came hot and fast, burning away the paralysis that often dogged her since Evan left. Flowers could not undo what Evan had done. They couldn't erase how he always vanished when she needed him, how he rationed his affection as if she didn't deserve it. Worse was the fury she turned inward, sharp and merciless. Why had she accepted his measly scraps of affection? The late replies and half-truths. The way she'd learned not to ask for more because asking made him retreat. She thought she was a great girlfriend. Doctors were busy—she knew that. But the truth was, it had felt safer to accept what little he offered than demand better.

She opened the envelope and withdrew the tiny flower card. The message was printed in neat, block letters.

Dear Jessica,
Welcome to the Stone family!!! We're so excited to meet you, and I'm dying to help plan your wedding too!
Cordially,
Mrs Abigail Stone

Jessica flipped the card back and forth. All the anger she had been wrestling with gave way to confusion. Was this from a patient? She couldn't recall and if it was, the message didn't make sense. Could it possibly be meant for someone else?

But there weren't any other doctors named Jessica working in her department. And it was impossible not to connect Nolan with the sender's last name. Abigail Stone. Nolan Stone.

So, who was Abigail Stone to Nolan? And why was she sending Jess flowers and wanting to plan her wedding?

She was bone-tired from working all night, but there was no way she could wait to get some answers. She grabbed the bouquet—it was heavy!—braced it against her hip and headed to Nolan's office.

No knock this time. She crossed the threshold and set the flowers on his desk. Hard.

"What's all this about?"

Nolan looked mystified at the flowers and the card she was pushing into his face. He withdrew the card, and Jess could have sworn he went two shades paler than normal.

He cleared his throat, then tucked the card back in its miniature envelope. "It appears my mother has sent you flowers."

"Why would she do that, Nolan?"

Nolan rubbed his brow, looking ill at ease. "She may be a bit confused."

"About?"

"My brother is getting married in a few weeks, and she believes I am bringing my fiancée to the wedding."

Jess cocked her head, feeling confused too. "You're getting married?"

"No, I'm not."

Jess pulled out the chair opposite his desk. "Explain."

Nolan shifted his weight, his gaze roaming the room and landing on anything but her. "Weddings make my mother very nostalgic and romantic. It makes her think of love and babies, and then she just can't help herself. She starts trying to get me matched up too."

He cleared his throat. "So, to put an end to her matchmaking, I may have…not exactly disagreed with her impression that I am getting married."

Her brows narrowed. "Nolan. That makes no sense. People don't just 'get an impression' that you're getting married. And why would she think *I'm* your fiancée?"

"No idea," he said. But then his brow furrowed and he turned to his computer. A few keystrokes later, he turned the screen her way.

"Maybe because of this."

He had pulled up the hospital's web page where pictures from a recent fundraiser had been posted. One featured him and Jess standing very close together. Jess remembered that shot and how the photographer had urged them to stand closer so she could include the hospital's donor board in the shot. He had smelled impossibly good—like fresh laundry and good decisions.

Jess studied the picture, including the caption where her name and department was identified. "Yeah, maybe." She rotated the screen back his way. "Questions, Nolan. I have many questions."

Which, judging from his dilated pupils and clenched jaw, he did not want to answer.

Nolan powered off the computer and closed the screen. A not-so-subtle hint that it was time for her to stop asking questions and take her leave. "I apologize for the confusion, Dr. Hayes. I will have this matter resolved very soon." He stood to open the door, indicating their meeting was over. "The flowers are yours to keep, of course."

Jess swallowed hard. Nolan's abrupt pivot back to work brushed against an old bruise, but she couldn't dwell on that. All that mattered was never again shrinking herself for someone else's convenience or comfort. She drew in a steadying breath, straightened her shoulders, and picked up the flowers. If Nolan didn't want to talk, that was fine, but she was leaving on her own terms.

She had crossed the threshold and was on her way to the elevator when Nolan called out.

"Unless…"

She turned back. "Unless?"

"The wedding will be in Napa Valley."

She cocked her head. "Yay?"

"At my family's vineyard."

Her eyes widened with obvious shock and disbelief. "You grew up on a vineyard?"

"Confirmed." His expression was maddeningly placid for a man who just admitted he won one of life's lotteries.

So, The Professor had a few secrets in his proverbial closet. Fake fiancées and family vineyards.

"You sly fox," she said, setting the flowers back on his desk, then dropping back into the chair. "Start talking, mister."

How that man hated to talk. It was obvious from the rigid set of his shoulders and how his fingers fidgeted with his cuffs. He'd probably be more enthusiastic if she just asked him to defuse a bomb with his stethoscope.

He coughed discreetly. "As I said, the wedding will be hosted at my family's vineyard in Napa Valley. I am told many people enjoy Napa Valley for weekend excursions. If you are one such person, I would, of course, cover all your expenses for the weekend."

"If I attend as your fiancée?"

His jaw was so tight, it practically quivered. "Ideally, yes."

Jess felt her body warm with delight. The heat settled in her chest and spiraled down her spine as she watched Nolan fidget and squirm. Every tiny movement screamed of his discomfort. She felt like a cat who had cornered her prey, and she wanted to draw out the delicious torture as long as possible.

She crossed her arms across her chest instead of bolting for the door. He couldn't hide the flicker of hope that sparked in his gaze.

"So, what kind of fiancée would Dr. Nolan Stone bring?"

Jess knew Nolan's real-world type pretty well by now. Tall leggy blondes, former cheerleaders and models who now worked as pharmaceutical reps or in public relations. All Jaguars and Jimmy

Choo. How they loved to fawn over The Professor. He didn't seem to mind the attention.

If that's who his family was expecting, her frizzy dark hair and short, athletic build was going to be a huge disappointment.

His gaze swept over her like a metal detector at security, sharp and impersonal. "Someone quiet. Reserved. Who uses the services of a personal shopper."

Oh, no. Absolutely not. What did Nolan think—that she was some kind of "before" picture in need of professional intervention? With a chuckle, she pushed to her feet and snagged the flowers, already halfway to the door before he could react. Time to teach Nolan a lesson. If he was shopping for a curated accessory, he'd clearly wandered into the wrong aisle.

"Okay, okay," he relented, waving to calm her. "Sit down."

She turned back his way, arched an eyebrow.

"Please?" he said. The word seemed difficult for him to articulate.

She set the flowers back on his desk and sat down.

"We are not the focal point of this weekend," Nolan continued. "So not much should be required of you beyond playing the role of my fiancée."

"And what would that entail?"

He threw up his hands in exasperation. "I don't

know, Dr. Hayes. Just don't throw anything heavy at my head. Is that manageable?"

Jess pretended to give it a good think. "I will try."

"So, do we have a deal?"

Jess knew she was savoring this unexpected, almost intimate, moment with Nolan way too much. But beyond her curiosity about the family who had produced Captain Clipboard, one question still burned in her chest.

"Why did you lie about having a fiancée?"

And just like that, the tiny thread of connection between them snapped. Nolan's gaze went dark with unspoken words.

"Honestly, Dr. Hayes," he said, his tone back to his clipped and precise cadence. "There's no need to hash out every minute detail of my *personal* life. The question is quite simple: Do you wish to enjoy a weekend in Napa Valley as my 'fiancée'—" he punctuated the word with air quotes, reminding her of her proper place in the equation "—or not?"

Jess felt tension coil in her chest, replacing her curiosity with tension and annoyance. He was back to his modus operandi: all jerk, no heart.

No way was she going to put herself on the line if he wasn't. If he wanted to keep her at arm's length, fine. But he would have to go to that wedding alone.

Evan had shown exactly how relationships built on emotional power imbalances ended—she would do all the reaching, the waiting, and the soothing while the man in front of her stayed conveniently unavailable. Even if this was just a fake engagement, she wasn't going into it as the weaker partner. Not for Nolan, or anyone else.

"As '*appealing*'—" she punctuated the word with her own angry air quotes "—as your proposal is, I'm afraid it violates Human Resources code 987654321, which expressly forbids fake engagements between employees of the Horizon Bay Medical Institute." She leaned back in her chair and pointlessly examined her fingernails. "I mean, the chances of us getting caught are slim, to be sure, but it's best to be…*prudent*, don't you think?"

It took a Herculean effort to keep her expression smooth and placid.

His smile was as dry and flimsy as tissue paper. His jaw tightened again—she was beginning to fear he'd develop lockjaw if he didn't cut that out.

"Quite right," he said, his expression settling back into the perfectly impassive wall she had banged her head against for the past year.

She felt a little spark at her win, tinged with a bit of regret. She rather enjoyed watching Nolan spend some time in the hot seat for a change.

"Home time for me," she said, heading for the door.

"Dr. Hayes."

She turned back.

"Your flowers."

She nodded and smiled, but he had already swiveled his chair so he could face the window.

She should feel happy. They were back in their zones, boxing gloves at the ready for their next sparring session. Instead, she just felt…a little sad.

Stop that, she scolded herself. She wasn't going to do this anymore. Men like Nolan were her Achilles heel. First her father, then Evan, but no more. She was done twisting herself into an emotional pretzel to win the affection and approval of emotionally unavailable men.

Mistakes were okay. But not learning from them? That was just stupid.

Jess punched the elevator button, bracing the flower vase against her hip. Damn, this thing was heavy. His mother had really gone all out to welcome Nolan's "fiancée" to the family.

Jess was a little sorry that this woman who was clearly trying to make a good first impression had missed the mark. But her timing was perfect, at least for Jess's purposes. She would be visiting her father at the rehab center later that day. This bouquet would make a nice addition to his stark room. Maybe it would even cheer him up a little.

The elevator took its sweet time getting to the seventh floor. It gave her mind time to wander. To think about vineyards and Napa Valley weddings.

As annoying as he could be, Jess couldn't deny being somewhat curious about her colleague too. What would Nolan be like away from the hospital? As far as dates went, she could do worse than The Professor. He *was* sort of handsome…in an annoyingly perfect, vintage-suit, martinis-solve-everything kind of way.

He'd wear a suit, of course. It was impossible to imagine Nolan in anything other than scrubs or a suit. But was he a single- or double-breasted kind of guy? Would he sport his usual, precise, disciplined hair part, or would he spike it up with a little gel?

She smiled despite herself, imagining Nolan in front of a mirror, messing with his hair until it was just right. That was enough to spark her imagination into full bloom. In a flash, she was thinking of the perfect dress for a Napa Valley wedding. Maybe a 1970s silk maxi dress with flowy bell sleeves and a flattering empire waist. Or maybe a vintage tea dress, sedate and virginal. Nolan's mother would love that…

Girl! Give it a rest!

She was *not* going to a Napa Valley wedding. She was *not* going to be anyone's fiancée. And she sure as hell wasn't shopping for dresses with Nolan's mother in mind!

Her father's voice rose up in her head, fond and gently exasperated, calling her a dreamer the way other people said *careful*. He'd always warned her about building castles out of maybes, about falling in love with the idea of what could be instead of dealing with what was standing right in front of her.

The elevator dinged and the steel doors slid open. Jess took a deep breath and stepped inside, then stabbed the ground floor button to return to the emergency department.

The doors slid shut, a symbolic closure to the most foolish idea she had ever entertained in her long list of foolish ideas.

Later that day, Jess had the impressive flower display centered on the dresser in her father's room at the Cedarbrook Rehabilitation Center.

"What do you think, Dad? They look nice, right?"

Her father tried to smile, but it was just a shadowy version of the jovial man he used to be. "Those are real pretty, Jess. But don't waste your money on flowers for me. They're just going to die."

Jess turned her back to him, so she could fuss with the flowers, arranging them just so because she didn't want him to detect the worry that was making her nibble at her bottom lip. Her father wasn't the same strong farmer she remembered from her youth. His movements had slowed, the easy strength she remembered replaced by careful, deliberate steps that made her chest tighten. He had once hauled feed sacks like they weighed nothing. His hands had smelled of sun and warm earth and easy certainty. Thoughts of what time was taking from him—and how she may have hastened his demise—left her feeling anxious and guilty.

When she felt more in control, she turned back and flashed him her brightest smile. "How's your day going so far, Dad?"

"Eh," he shrugged. "Not bad. But that terrible woman keeps stopping by. I think she wants to torture me."

Jess bit back a smile. "That's your physical therapist, Dad, and she's not torturing you. At least not on purpose. She's trying to help you get stronger so you can go home."

As usual, his room was in pristine condition: his books stacked just so, not a stray sock or paper in sight. You could take the man out of the military, but it wasn't so easy to take the military out of the man.

Jess had tried to soften things up, bringing blankets from home, a picture of her mother, some board games they could play when she visited. But he put everything in the closet, except for the picture of her mother.

Who was she kidding? She could never make this clean, sterile room feel like home. The sprawling Midwestern farm of her childhood was long gone, along with the memories of her father with his hands deep in the soil, coaxing life from the earth. Home for him was a weathered barn packed with farm equipment that he could tinker back to life. An old-fashioned kitchen with peeling linoleum and strong coffee on the stove. Not a medical rehab center where his schedule consisted of physical therapy, yoga classes, and bingo.

When he had gotten injured, she had thought it was best to sell the farm and move him closer to her in San Francisco where she could help. Now she wondered if she hadn't been looking out for herself too. She had moved to San Francisco a year earlier, where she knew no one in the crowded, bustling city. Maybe loneliness and feeling homesick had made her vulnerable to Evan's charismatic attention. When her father broke his hip shortly after Evan left for Florida, it seemed only natural to move him closer so she could help.

But now, seeing how the move had stripped him of the passions that gave his life shape and meaning, she wondered if her motivations had been selfish. Her father was the only family she had in the world. Maybe she had only moved him here so she wouldn't feel so alone.

She shook off her regrets and fears, wanting to focus on something that might bring a spark of life back to her father's eyes.

The physical therapist had left a handout of exercises, but the paper lay untouched on his nightstand. Try as she might, she could not get him to attempt them. Her father was depressed in his new city, and especially in the rehab facility. Her goal was to help him get well enough to come and live with her, but who was she kidding? How would a man like her father be happy in a small apartment with a terrace? She told herself that they would find something he would like. Maybe a small home in the suburbs, or a trailer on a half acre of land. But those options sounded like a poor consolation prize compared to what he had lost.

Her unsuccessful negotiations with her father after her strange encounter with Nolan left her weary. She needed a little break to stretch her legs and find something to drink. Maybe when she got back, they could take a little walk on the gentle path that wound through the facility's gardens. If he couldn't tend his own land, maybe he could at least enjoy someone else's.

She returned a few minutes later, bringing some snacks back. There was a nursing assistant in the room now, and she had moved the flowers from the dresser to a table near the window.

"Such lovely flowers for your father!" she said, fussing with the blooms.

Jess was about to answer when she noticed something in her father's hands. It was the flower card, already removed from its envelope.

In slow motion, Jess realized what was happening, but was powerless to stop it. The nursing assistant had assumed the flowers were for him and had naturally given him the card. Jess stood frozen in the doorway, watching helplessly as her father's pale blue eyes scanned the text.

Then he looked at her, his eyes so full of spark and light, she felt almost dazzled.

"Jessie-Bug…you're getting married?"

Jess's mouth opened, but no sound came out.

She knew what she should say. *Oh, heavens no. Just a little mix-up at work. It's all getting straightened out.*

But in the time it took for her to process that thought, she could see something new. Or rather, something old and familiar.

Not a rehab room that smelled faintly of disinfectant and overcooked vegetables. Or the walker parked too close to the bed.

Her father. Just like the old days. Strong and bright, looking at her with the same spark in his eyes she remembered from her childhood. The spark she hadn't seen since before surgery and recovery and physical therapy schedules.

She crossed the room slowly, stopping at the side of his bed, one hand sliding around the rail.

"Um, no," she said.

His smile faltered. Her stomach dropped.

She closed her eyes for half a beat, willing herself to tell him the truth. But it was just too easy to recalibrate and search for the least damaging option.

Telling him the truth now meant watching that light fade from his eyes. Chasing the color out of his cheeks and erasing the small smile that she hadn't seen for months.

If a patient were this fragile, she thought, *would you rip away the one thing making them want to get out of bed tomorrow?*

She nodded toward the card in his hand. "I mean, not yet. Nothing is scheduled yet."

Jess gave a small, helpless breath of a laugh. It wasn't a lie, exactly. Just not the whole truth.

He blinked, processing. "Well, that's all right!" That spark flickered again, bright and stubborn. "That gives me more time to recover, so I can walk you down the aisle."

Jess closed her eyes against her regret. She should end this right here. Be a good daughter.

But for the first time in months, her father looked like the man she remembered. A man who could and would fight his way back to himself.

Her chest tightened. What should a good daughter do?

In the end, her father's jovial smile decided the matter for her.

Because if a harmless ruse gave him something to reach for, she wasn't sure she had the will to take that away.

Nolan should have known better than to answer the phone.

A storm had been brewing all morning, leaving the sky with black and purple bruises. By midday, rain was battering the windows of Nolan's office in sporadic bursts. The kind that made the lights flicker and the room feel crackly with electricity. Thunder rolled in the distance, moving ever closer.

The ominous approach of the storm merged with a familiar tightening in his chest as he recognized his father's number. He should let it go to voicemail. It would be better to hear what his father wanted before he responded. But habit won out over instinct, as it usually did when it came to his father.

"Son," his father said, his tone somehow both warm and imperial. "Your brother and I were just talking about the wedding. I thought we should keep you in the play."

Nolan leaned into his desk, his eyes finding the barest imprint of a stain on the polished wood. *Keep him in the play.* Of course. His father had always loved the clean lines of professional sports where, as he said, everyone knew what their job was. Make the play. Win the game. Take one for the team when necessary.

Apparently settling down was the newest play expected of the Stone boys.

"I can't tell you what it means to your mother and me," his father continued, "seeing both our boys settled. You both have successful careers, and now are on the verge of starting families of your own. Feels like we did something right."

His words landed softly, which somehow made them hit harder. That was the problem. His father's praise was rare, but impactful. And it often came like this—quiet and heavy with expectation.

His father was proud of him because he thought he was settling down. As if a fiancée were the final credential he'd been missing.

"We're looking forward to getting your fiancée in the lineup," his father said, a hint of a smile in his voice. "Your mother's already talking about seating charts. Wants to make sure she feels welcome."

Nolan's grip tightened on the phone. He stared at the wall, letting his gaze settle on an abstract painting he had mounted opposite his desk. The pale color and clean lines appealed to him for its deliberate simplicity. The kind of art that made him feel order was possible.

Nolan's thumb found a chip on the edge of his desk and couldn't stop working it. His father's lack of assumption or agenda made all of this worse. Why had he let his vague comment morph into this hopeful expectation? He had told himself he was just buying himself time, but now he was facing a full-blown mess.

Just tell him. Right now.

"I'm…looking forward to it," Nolan said carefully.

"Good," his father replied. "It'll be nice, seeing you happy."

Then the line clicked and Nolan was alone, staring at his phone in a sort of stunned disbelief. When had his father ever wanted to just "see him happy"? Happiness had never been the goal when his father woke him at 4:00 a.m. in a vain attempt to get his youngest boy in "football shape." It had been about driving, sacrificing, winning, and changing. His father had been so certain that if he invested enough time, and Nolan did the hard work, he could be a football star just like his brother. Not that anyone had ever asked him if that's what he wanted.

After the call ended, the room felt too quiet. Nolan sat there longer than necessary, phone still in his hand, pulse ticking behind his eyes. His father was happy because he thought Nolan was happy. Nolan knew how to live his life by checking off the boxes his father thought were important. But this side of his father—emotional and agenda free—was new territory for him.

For the first time, Nolan wished he was bringing a fiancée for real. Just so he could feel like this connection with his father was real too.

He exhaled slowly, wracking his brain for the solution. There *had* to be one. He just hadn't found it yet.

His musings were interrupted by the shrill call of his pager.

ED requesting consult. Dr. Hayes, Bay 12. Male, 18, headache. Possible petechia.

Jess again. Of course. What better way to muddle his day than an interaction with Dr. Jessica Hayes.

He grabbed his white coat and headed to the emergency room. It was hopping busy today: A summer thunderstorm could do that. The waiting room was full of anxious parents, sprained ankles from wet sidewalks, and car crash victims. So many car crashes.

Jess was waiting outside Bay 12, her arms crossed tight. "Thanks for coming. I've got Jack here, an eighteen-year-old male who came in with a bad headache. Everything else seems normal—except for a single petechia on his big toe."

"Just one?" He was already frowning. Sure, the tiny red spots of petechiae *could* be an indicator of a very serious medical condition, but most of the time they meant nothing.

"Does he have a cough to go with that headache?"

Jess shook her head vigorously. "I know what you're thinking. I've ruled out all the fun reasons for petechiae. He doesn't have a cold and he's not taking any medications."

Nolan reviewed Jess's assessment and tests in Jack's electronic medical record. Everything looked normal.

"Jess, I don't know…" He trailed off. Her expression—tight, pale, and worried—concerned him more than the boy at this moment. Jess could annoy the bejesus out of him with her perpetually sunny moods, but she wasn't prone to dramatics.

"Okay, I'll take a look."

He stepped into the room, giving Jack a far more thorough exam than his medical record indicated he needed. He lifted the boy's limbs, checked his reflexes, examined his spine, and then looked over every inch of the skin, searching for signs of trouble. There was nothing to find. No rash. No fever. No stiff neck. Just a bad headache and one tiny spot on his toe.

He stepped back out to confer with Jess. "I'm not finding anything that would warrant more testing," he said carefully. "A spinal tap, full labs.... It's just a lot to ask, Jess." Unnecessary tests could traumatize a healthy kid, fracture a family's trust, and ripple through the department as another example of overreach.

Jess grabbed his sleeve, hard. "Nolan! When's the last time you had an eighteen-year-old boy bring himself to the ED?"

He blinked in response. She was doing it again, muddying up the road to diagnosis with feelings and possibilities. Part of him bristled at the uncertainty she embraced so naturally. His need for data and evidence clashing with her desire to trust her instincts.

And yet, he couldn't deny that her gut had steered them right more than once. Which made it harder to dismiss her concerns about this boy.

He looked back at Jack, then at Jess. The risks were high here. If he authorized expensive testing and it turned out to be a run-of-the-mill headache, he'd be called to the chief of pediatrics office to justify every line item, every decision.

But if he released the boy, and Jess was right…

He exhaled the breath he didn't know he was holding. "All right. Order the labs. I'll call neuro."

After that, everything moved very fast. Neurology signed off on the spinal tap, which went smoothly, but the labs that followed did not. Jack had an elevated white blood cell count and abnormal cerebrospinal fluid. Classic markers for bacterial meningitis, a very dangerous infection.

Jess's instincts had been right on, even though Jack's diagnostic criteria didn't warrant alarm. Nolan felt a surge of mixed emotions. He was relieved the boy would be okay but also struggling with a sort of panicky relief that Jess had not allowed his reliance on protocols to override her intuition. Those "gut feelings" that so often annoyed him had just saved a life.

By the time they had the full picture, Jack was crashing: His oxygen level plummeted and his vitals tanked. Thanks to Jess's instincts, the boy was in the pediatric ICU by then, safe in the care of a team of dedicated doctors and nurses.

A neurologist left the PICU and clapped Nolan on the shoulder. "Good call," he said. "He was less than an hour from crashing and dying."

Without hesitation, Nolan glanced Jess's way. "All the credit goes to Jess. She pushed for more testing."

"And saved his life," the neurologist said with a warm smile. "Well done, Dr. Hayes."

Jess hovered near the nurses' station, seeming unable to leave until Jack was truly stabilized.

Nolan touched her elbow lightly. "Come on, Hayes. Let's go write this up before the administration starts breathing down our necks."

She followed him to his office, still shaken. The storm outside was getting worse. The rain hammered the windows like some sort of coordinated attack.

It felt like déjà vu, her sitting across from him again. But this time without a huge vase of flowers and a lot of attitude between them.

"Why did you change your mind?" she asked.

That was easy. A lot easier than explaining why he would make up a fake fiancée to bring to his superstar athlete brother's wedding.

"Because you were right," he said. And she had been. Recognizing her talent in the ED had never been an issue for him. It was all the other…static… she brought that clouded his mind and confused his senses.

She stared at him as if she were trying to figure something out. He felt decidedly on the spot, like a specimen under a microscope.

His computer pinged, then his mother's image popped up.

She was video calling him. No doubt this was follow-up to the discussion he had had with his father earlier.

His stomach lurched. Oh, why hadn't he gotten that damn email done? More days had slipped by and now he *really* had to tell the truth. Only this time it would be face-to-face.

Jess glanced at the screen, then at him. Her head cocked ever so slightly. "Is that your mom?"

He swallowed and fessed up. "Yeah."

She studied him harder, but there was something soft in her gaze. "You still want to do that thing we talked about?"

There was something hesitant, almost vulnerable, in her expression. Some feeling rose in him before he had the power to squelch it back down. Some strange pulse of wanting to make this arrangement more personal, and it sucked the breath right out of him.

Before he could sort it all out, Jess leaned forward, her eyes glinting with mischief.

"Okay, I'll do it. But!" She raised a finger for emphasis, and Nolan held his breath, waiting for the proverbial shoe to drop. "I get to pick your shirt and tie for the wedding."

Nolan blinked as he tried to process her request. Why would she want to choose his attire for the wedding? Curiosity soon gave way to dread as memories of her always flamboyant, never sedate or tasteful, collection of scrubs struck genuine fear in his heart. What on earth would she choose for him? Unwanted images of fluorescent pink flamingoes flooded his brain.

This was a terrible concession. Potentially humiliating. And yet, rather modest considering she would be sacrificing a weekend of her life for his benefit.

The video call kept ringing. His mother was waiting for an explanation.

Pink flamingoes, he decided, were infinitely better than his mother's third degree.

"Fine," he surrendered, trying not to choke on the word. Jess smirked as the ringtone chimed again.

He reached for the trackpad but stopped when her hand shot out to close over his. Her warm, smooth skin sent a shock of electricity up his arm so fast, he forgot how to breathe.

"One more thing," she said. And then she spoke so rapid-fire, he could hardly process her words. "You have to be *my* fiancé when we visit my father."

He froze, felt his mouth fall agape. "Why would you need…"

Before he could finish, she reached across the desk and pressed the accept button.

"Mrs. Stone! I am so pleased to meet you!" Jess

sang out, her tone instantly warm and bright and charming. "Thank you so much for the flowers. They were gorgeous!"

Nolan watched his mother adjust her glasses and burst into a genuine, warm smile. "Jessica Hayes, is that you? I have been *dying* to meet you and…"

Nolan watched in a state of stunned disbelief as the two of them chatted warmly. Jess effortlessly, seamlessly, wove a conversation with her mother, built around the wedding and books and recipes, and the weather. As if Jess had been part of the family for years.

In the back of his mind, the gears ground slowly. Had she planned this all along? Knowing she needed him for a favor but setting things up so he wouldn't ask too many questions about why *she* needed a fake fiancé too?

It was possible. More than possible.

Jessica Hayes was unpredictable, disarming, and ridiculously good at pushing every button he had.

Even so, she was unraveling the one problem he hadn't been able to solve in weeks.

He could handle this. He just needed to brace himself for the chaos she always brought in her wake.

He leaned back slowly, feeling the power of the storm blend with Jess's laughter as she worked her magic on his mother. All brightness and warmth and ease.

He wasn't feeling in control of much at the moment.

But for the first time since this fiasco had begun, it seemed possible that his life might just get back to normal.

CHAPTER THREE

JESS HAD BEEN bracing herself to hate Nolan's car long before it pulled up. The text he'd sent was a reminder of his all-business, no-charm personality.

Meet me out front at 2 p.m. Silver Audi S8 with laser headlights. Ring shopping at Regalia & Co.

That was fine by her. She didn't have time for distractions either. She had schedules to keep, patients to check on, and a checklist of real priorities that didn't include pretending to be his fiancée for longer than absolutely necessary. The last thing she wanted to do was spend some of her precious free time in his German spaceship of a car to one of San Francisco's most exclusive jewelry stores.

The temptation to shoot back with her own text was strong.

How 'bout we take BART downtown, hit up a few pawn shops for a ring, then chow down on some food truck tacos?

But with monumental restraint, she let the urge pass. As if Nolan would ever take the train! The wedding was just two weeks away. That plus visiting her father meant she just had to get through this charade for a few weeks. Besides, she wasn't doing this for Nolan's sake. Ever since her father read that flower card, his whole demeanor had changed. According to his caseworker's weekly reports, he was working out like a senior Olympic athlete almost every day. All so he could walk his daughter down the aisle at her wedding.

She slid her phone into her pocket as a sedan pulled up. It was just as gray and boxy and snobbish as she expected.

"Nice car," she said, sliding into the buttery leather seat.

He ignored her dry tone but dialed the radio volume higher, filling the car's cabin with an orchestral thunderous crescendo. The relentless cascade of strings and percussion as they navigated the streets of San Francisco left no room for conversation, which she had to admit was probably a wise decision on Nolan's part.

Even from the parking lot, Regalia & Co. shimmered under the July sun. Its brushed steel, floor-to-ceiling glass, and impressive revolving door made it look like a palace. A doorman in a perfectly pressed suit bowed slightly as he opened the door for a woman pushing a narrow purple stroller. As they passed, Jess could see a miniature poodle tucked inside, its ear bows and collar coordinated to match the stroller.

For crying out loud...

Nolan parked the car and dashed to her side to open the door.

She ignored his extended hand. "Save it for the wedding, big guy."

"Never too early to practice," he said, aiming his key fob over his shoulder and locking the door with a sharp beep.

The jewelry store was just as opulent inside. A huge crystal chandelier hung overhead, and the thick, plush carpeting muted their footfalls. A tall, thin woman in a black tailored suit met them at the door, introducing herself as their jewelry concierge. She ushered them to a private viewing room where they were offered wine, espresso, or house-brewed pomegranate tea, which Jess refused because it would be just her luck to knock her drink over and embarrass herself in this posh setting.

The selection of rings was…fine. Sterile, precise, and entirely unsurprising—just like Nolan himself. None of them spoke of imagination, of quirks, of a story worth telling; they were polished and safe, designed to impress rather than delight. They felt like something a woman who measured life in checklists and color-coded closets would swoon over, not someone who noticed the little sparks in the world—or in a man.

"Would you like to try one on?" the concierge asked with maximum politeness.

Her expression must have betrayed her, because Nolan asked her what was wrong.

"Well, they're just a little…boring."

The concierge's posture visibly stiffened.

Nolan shot the stern woman a reassuring smile, then leaned close to whisper. "What does that matter? We just need something to help you fit in with my family, that's all."

Fitting in. She hated that phrase. It reminded her of Evan, who had spent months dispensing advice on how to "improve" herself under the guise of mentoring her career. All the while hiding the truth about his own life—his lies, his double-dealing, the way he'd lived a whole other existence while lecturing her on honesty and ambition.

Oh, what did it matter what ring she wore? This was Nolan's family and Nolan's problem. She was just an actress in this play.

She shook her head to get herself sorted. "Never mind. Pick whatever ring you want."

"Well, then…" His gaze scanned the rings that the concierge had presented on a velvet pillow, each angled just right so they would catch the light. He plucked the last one and studied it under the light. "I think this one is perfect for you."

Okay, that was the *one* ring that wasn't too cringey. He handed it to her and she felt the warmth from his fingers lingering in the platinum band.

"It's…interesting," she conceded. The ring felt light and honest in her hand, and the tiny amethyst stones provided a subtle pop of color that made it feel alive. Unlike the others, it didn't try to impress, even though it had a personality of its own. That made it feel more special somehow.

"That's from our *Lumen Vitae* collection," the concierge said. "Latin for Light of Life. You've chosen the Firefly design. Notice the subtle amethyst wings framing the diamond? They're designed to catch the light and add a touch of color."

Jess turned the ring from side to side. "You had me at firefly wings."

"How charming," the concierge said with a tight smile.

Nolan only smiled, unbothered. "I just figured you would prefer something more…exotic."

"Excellent," the concierge purred. "There are a number of wedding bands that will pair well with that ring." She took the ring back from Jess, then paused before returning it to its black velvet ring box. She plucked her glasses from where they were perched on her head, and examined the ring.

"It appears this ring has a loose prong in the design. We could have this repaired in a few days, or you could make another selection?"

Nolan arched an eyebrow in Jess's direction. "New selection," he said, at the exact same moment that Jess said, "Repair, please."

The concierge's gaze swept back and forth between them.

Nolan deferred to Jess with a magnanimous wave of his hand. "Whatever the lady prefers."

"Repair, please," Jess repeated.

"Absolutely." The concierge picked up the tray of engagement rings and turned to leave, then paused at the door. "You may be happy to know that we offer a thirty-day return period on our engagement rings, so long as they have not been resized or damaged."

The door closed with a quiet click. Nolan glanced at Jess. "Doesn't sound like she thinks we'll make it to the wedding."

"Can't imagine why not. With our just-a-couple-crazy-kids-in-love vibe?"

"Your perpetual scowl does send a different message, that's for sure."

"Oh, really?" Jess's temper flared. "Maybe if you weren't so bossy and..." Her retort trailed off as she took in his weary expression. Yeah, they were at it again.

"If we can't convince a total stranger that we're crazy in love..." he began.

"How will we convince those who know us best?" she finished.

He paced over to the small window that looked out to San Francisco's busy streets. Then he turned back to her, his jaw tight and his lips pressed into a thin, flat line.

"Practice," was his answer. "We'll just have to practice being a couple that appears to actually like each other."

He came back to where she sat. Then coughed like he had something stuck in his throat. "Would you care to join me for a romantic lunch to celebrate our recent engagement?"

Something rose from deep in her gut that felt like a wall of fire. Practicing and romantic lunch were not supposed to be part of their ruse. This was supposed to be a simple arrangement. Something that wouldn't require too much of her free time or attention.

Behind that thought, there was something else. A tiny spark of anticipation that left her feeling uneasy. What would it mean to spend time away from work with The Professor?

Jess knew she could be a dreamer, but she wasn't an idiot. Evan had taught her all she needed to know about character, loyalty, and the risks of dating colleagues. There was no way she would fall for Nolan, even if he was her type, which he definitely was not.

"Okay, fine," she said, shooting her hand out to shake his, initiating their truce. "But I get to pick the restaurant."

Nolan knew he would hate Jess's choice for a restaurant as soon as she told him to look up The Sushi Loop on his GPS.

Consuming raw fish had never appealed to him. And that was *before* he became a doctor and treated a parade of kids for food poisoning, thanks to undercooked meat at family barbecues or pizza that had been left out too long.

So opting—of his own free will—to eat fish that had never seen the hot side of a frying pan? That would be a hard no. Still, he found himself agreeing, because he could see how thin her patience was as they discussed engagement rings. The last thing he wanted was to push her to the point where she decided this arrangement cost more than it was worth.

His opinion did not improve once they had been seated at a booth. In many ways, The Sushi Loop was like any other restaurant—a bright, bustling place with busy servers delivering drinks and desserts. With one big difference—there was a narrow metal conveyor belt running adjacent to their table, presenting a parade of sushi options on tiny colorful plates.

Jess plucked two plates of California rolls from the conveyor belt as soon as they were seated.

He wrinkled his nose. "Where have you taken me?"

"It's a kaiten sushi restaurant," she explained, pouring soy sauce over her rolls. "You've never been?"

He held his hand over the conveyor belt, where

plates of who-knows-what whizzed by, testing the temperature. "This food isn't being kept chilled!"

She shrugged. "I eat here all the time. It hasn't killed me yet," she said before popping a roll in her mouth.

Nolan watched her pluck two more plates from the belt, utterly mystified at what made this woman tick. She had to be the biggest walking oxymoron he had ever met.

He reached for a menu. "I can't quite reconcile how an emergency room doctor, who has seen every variation of *it hasn't killed me yet* gone wrong, can be so nonplussed about acquiring a nasty case of botulism."

She smiled, unwrapping a pair of chopsticks. "Well, you're right. There's a lot of possibilities here. We *could* get food poisoning…"

"Or salmonella…listeria…"

"Or…" she continued, poking her chopsticks at him to emphasize the word. "You could like it so much that you spend all your free time inventing a chilled conveyor belt system. Then you patent your idea and make millions. Anything could happen!" She leaned closer and whispered, "Even something good."

That familiar urge to snipe a pithy retort was strong, more out of habit than genuine annoyance. But that would only make her snipe back, and then they'd be right back where they were at the jewelry store.

"Thanks, but I limit my gambling to lottery tickets."

The waiter stopped at their table and he ordered teriyaki chicken from the menu, a dish that would be cooked and served at bacteria-destroying temperatures.

He shifted his attention back to Jess, who was pulling two more dishes from the conveyor belt. Whatever it was, it still had eyes. He shuddered. "I've been thinking about our situation. If we're going to be a convincing engaged couple, I think we'll need a few ground rules."

She studied him with a deadpan expression. "You don't say."

He refused to take the bait, even though the familiar tug to overexplain scratched at him. The restaurant hummed around them—low voices, clink of silverware. Nolan folded his hands on the table to anchor himself.

"I'm thinking three simple rules should keep us out of trouble. One, be nice. Two, don't talk too much. And three, don't insult each other in public."

Her eyes widened, sharp and offended. "I would never do that!"

Disbelief cut through his resolve, vaporizing his recent vow to stay calm. He felt it then—the tight, jittery energy she always stirred in him, equal parts irritation and intrigue. "You do it all the time!"

"Name one example!"

Without breaking a sweat, he rattled off a half dozen examples. "What about that time you told the nurses I color-coded my stethoscopes?"

"Are you saying you don't?"

"I only have one!" He leaned back in his seat, his pulse ticking faster than he liked. "Or mocking how I organize the supply closet?"

"Nolan! You alphabetize the bandages!"

"I do not," he snapped back, heat creeping up his neck even as he clocked the amused glances from a nearby table. "They're arranged by height."

Even as the words left his mouth, he knew exactly how this must look—a couple on a date, bickering over organizational principles like it was a life-or-death matter. Still, he couldn't seem to extricate himself from the fight.

"And just a few days ago…what did you say? That I need to lighten up?"

She rolled her eyes. "I *said* you need to learn to go with the flow. That's not an insult. That's just plain truth."

He felt it again. That hot feeling in his chest that always rose when he and Jess got started. Heat warmed his face and his body buzzed with some kind of thought-jamming electricity that made his words come out all wrong.

Dammit, they were off track again. He forced himself to take a deep breath, then held up his hand to signal his conditional surrender in this battle.

"Never mind—it doesn't matter. Rules or no rules…whatever. We just have to figure out how to play nice for a few days."

"Fine. What do you suggest?"

"Let's practice a simple conversation." He held up a warning finger. "Without snark."

She fussed with her napkin and muttered something about people having no sense of adventure.

He arched an eyebrow. She crossed her arms and rolled her eyes.

"Fine." She looked out the window, then back at him. "Nice weather we're having."

"Really?"

"Well, you try!"

He considered what might be safe territory. Work was certainly out—they clashed there constantly. Their personal lives…seemed tricky, but that was all they had left outside the weather.

"So, what do you do outside of work? Any hobbies? Sports?"

"When I'm not at work, I visit my father at his rehab center. I volunteer at a cat shelter when I can and I like to train for and run marathons."

Well. That was a surprise. But it did explain the legs.

When he had picked Jess up at the hospital, she had changed from scrubs into her street clothes. Today it was a gypsy-like dress with a plethora of colors swirled into an abstract pattern that invited an optical migraine. *Typical Jess*, he had thought. *All flair and drama and glitter and wow.*

But the dress also showed off her legs. And now, when she shifted her legs away from the table, her dress fell open, revealing the slope of her calf and a delicate ankle bracelet.

Dr. Jessica Hayes had legs. Rather nice legs, actually.

He gave himself a mental shake. She was doing it again, diverting him from the task at hand. Why was this woman so damn distracting?

She folded her hands on the table, prim like a schoolgirl. "What do *you* do when you aren't at work?"

Precious little would be the honest answer. Once Nolan understood that his father's approval was something to be earned through success, he had poured himself into academics with the same single-minded focus that his father had demanded in their athletic practices.

Starting college at fourteen had sealed his fate. He was fluent in his studies and a rock star in the lab but awkward everywhere else. The hospital had become his refuge, a place where his efforts translated into clean outcomes, and his long work hours felt safer than parties, small talk, or the risk of getting some human interaction wrong.

"Krav Maga," he finally settled on. "It's a modern combat and self-defense system."

For the first time since he had met Jess, her eyebrows raised in surprise. Which pleased him more than he expected.

"You don't seem like the fighting type," Jess said.

Nolan huffed a quiet breath. "I'm not. Not in the way you're thinking." He hesitated, then added, "My dad and my brother are both very gifted athletes. My father played professional football for eight years, then Connor followed in his footsteps. They're big, loud, all muscle and instinct." He steepled his hands in front of his face, creating a little distance between him and Jess. "Despite my father's best efforts, I was…not that."

Jess's expression hitched for just a moment. Her gaze lingered on his face and he saw a slight softening in the corners of her mouth. She nodded for him to continue.

"In Krav Maga, none of that matters. It's about control. Staying steady when everything in you wants to panic. Being disciplined in practice so you can stay upright when the pressure hits."

Something in Jess's expression shifted, the edge softening. "So, that's why you practically have every hospital protocol memorized."

He shrugged and smiled. "It keeps things from getting messy."

She studied him for a beat longer than necessary, as if fitting this new piece into place. The smile that followed was more thoughtful. "Hey—we're doing pretty good so far. What's next?"

"We need to get our backstories straight for the wedding. How we met, when we started dating… that sort of thing."

"Oh goody." She wriggled in her seat with anticipation. "I've been thinking about this too. I have ideas, Nolan. So many ideas!"

He withdrew a paper folded in thirds from his coat pocket. Followed by a pen. "As do I. So, I took the liberty of creating a document to organize our ideas."

Jess sighed. "Of course you did." She craned to see the paper and read aloud. "Timeline. Anecdotes. Absolutely Not." She cocked her head in the form of a question.

"Timeline is where we figure out when we met, started dating, that sort of thing. Anecdotes are funny stories we'll share if we need them. And Absolutely Not is our no-go zone. Lies we can't tell because they are too hard to maintain or remember. So," he uncapped his pen. "Let's start with something easy. Where we met." He leaned forward to write *Met at work* under the timeline.

Jess wrinkled her nose. "*Borrring*. How 'bout this? You crashed into me in a parking garage. You didn't have your registration paperwork, so the police arrested you for grand theft." She clasped her hands under her chin. "I was shattered by your soulful brown eyes, so I bailed you out. You bought me breakfast at a twenty-four-hour diner. Then we walked the streets of San Francisco, arm in arm, sipping lattes and watching the city come to life, the smell of fresh-baked sourdough scenting the air…"

"The entire city smelled like sourdough?"

She gazed at some spot over his shoulder, her eyes unfocused and dreamy. "Yeah…"

He shook his head hard, mostly to remind himself who he was dealing with. "No, Jess. Just…no."

"Why not?"

"Because no one would ever believe I would operate a motor vehicle without my license and registration."

Her dreamy expression faded. "Good point." She captured another sushi roll with her chopsticks. "What if I got into an accident…"

She trailed off as he wrote *Motor Vehicle Stories* in the Absolutely Not column. Then underlined *Met at work* three times.

"Oh, Nolan. That is so bor…"

"I know—boring. But it's also easy to remember. And not likely to lead to many follow-up questions when we are apart."

She nodded. "Okay, we met at work. But…how did you ask me out?"

Her expectant expression made him nervous.

"Well, I found you during your shift…"

She shrugged, unimpressed. "Conventional start, but that's okay. What did you say?"

A familiar wave of frustration waved over him. Social situations always left him feeling off balance, and romantic ones were even worse—full of invisible rules he never quite understood.

Jess was watching him expectantly, clearly envisioning something cinematic, and the pressure made his mind go blank. This mattered to her; he understood that much, even if he didn't understand *why*.

"Um," he said at last, defaulting to the one version of himself that never failed him, "I suppose I would've said something like, 'Dr. Hayes, I understand MedTech Innovations is hosting a lecture this Friday on advancements in pediatric airway stabilization.'"

Her eyebrows hitched considerably.

"I thought perhaps we could have dinner and attend the lecture together." He folded his hands on the table, satisfied.

Jess waited a moment before throwing her arms across the back of her seat with a dramatic, audible yawn.

Nolan stared at her, torn between irritation and reluctant amusement. He recognized her familiar tactic immediately—a mix of exaggeration and theatrical impatience that once would have sent him retreating into silence. But this time, a huff of laughter escaped him before he could stop it.

"I'm sorry," he said dryly, rubbing a hand over his face, "was that not sweeping enough for you?"

"No, *Nolan*, it was not," she said, drawing out the syllables of his name. "No one would ever believe I would attend an educational seminar on a Friday night."

"But my family doesn't even know you."

"Nolan," she said, her tone firm. "Look at me. Do I look like I would spend a Friday night at a medical lecture?"

And so he did. And that was when he realized how hard he tried to *not* stare at her at work for the past six months since he joined the staff at Horizon Bay. How he would focus on her forehead when they conferred, just to avoid the pull of her deep blue eyes. Or zone in on her nose, so his eyes wouldn't trace the sensuous curve of her mouth. Or find reasons to study the ceiling when she walked away, so he wouldn't be hypnotized by the rhythmic sway of her hips.

But now, he couldn't *not* see her. The deep red lipstick she wore made him think of Merlot. Her silver dangly earrings glittered like tiny disco balls in the light. The flowy, jewel-toned dress in shades of emerald and sapphire played off the cerulean blue of her eyes.

She was right. No man in his right mind would take her to an educational lecture on a Friday night.

She waved her hand impatiently, ready to move on. "Never mind—let's skip ahead. How did you ask me to marry you? Don't be shy, Nolan. Go big with it!"

She leaned back in the booth, clearly expecting

a spectacular story. He felt his palms go a little clammy.

"We dated for three months and then we got engaged."

She licked her lips and nodded, urging him on. "Okay…"

He blinked twice.

She waited, then waited some more. "Wait, that's it? The End?"

"It fits with the timeline just right and it's believable!"

"Cripes, Nolan. No one goes to a wedding wanting *believable*."

"But we're not the ones getting married!"

"That doesn't matter. This is a weekend of romantic fantasy. When guests show up for a wedding, they're expecting the free buffet, open bar, and a generous serving of Love Conquers All. Every detail and experience is designed to renew our faith in humanity and endless love. Nothing will kill that fantasy faster than being *believable*."

Nolan swiped a hand through his hair, thoroughly exasperated. None of his plans were working out. But why would they? His love life had never been easy—he didn't know the rules of the game. He was honest to the point of awkwardness and completely transparent. So far, that had led to a pretty lackluster track record. "Well, what would you say? Start with how we met, keeping it in the 'actually possible' category."

She paused to think, her gaze assessing him from head to toe. He sat a little straighter, hoping he was passing whatever test she was giving him.

She mused aloud, her gaze unfocused. "We met when I stole your patient." She paused, then smiled. "Yeah, that's a good meet-cute for us."

"A meet what? And that's not a story. You *are* always stealing my patients."

"Not stealing…borrowing. And only when I have new interns to train in the ED."

"Yeah? Well, your semantics are making my patient metrics go down in flames."

She smiled again. She was back in her dream world. "We collaborated on the case. Long nights in the medical library. Early morning meetings at the patient's bedside led to…"

Despite himself, he got absorbed in the story. "My admiration for your…unorthodox methods… grew…"

She opened her eyes. "Nolan! That's the nicest fake compliment you've ever given me." She folded her hands under her chin. "Now, how did you propose to me? Take your time. Think glitter, sparkles, bonfires…at the beach! We could say…"

He held up a hand to stop her so he could think. He wracked his brain, trying to come up with something that would impress Jess. But all that came to mind was making a reservation at a proper restaurant with cloth napkins and live piano, followed by champagne and a proper proposal speech.

"What about a sunset proposal?" she offered helpfully. "Maybe a hot air balloon?"

Absolutely not.

"Fireworks then."

Illegal.

"Oh, wait. Would we be too retro if we say you hired a flash mob?"

Nolan shook his head, rubbing his temples where he felt a familiar headache sneaking up on him again.

"Okay, fine. Let's go with something more Nolan-esque." She leaned forward and folded her arms on the table, making her dress fall open. A teasing hint of black lace made his throat go dry. "We were in the on-call room and you brought me a coffee from the cafe downstairs."

That was a good start, but his shoulders hiked up an inch as he braced for the ambush. Surely there would be a basket of puppies or an aerial marriage proposal coming next.

"You even spelled my name right on the cup. That's when I knew it was true love."

After several long seconds, he released the breath he had been holding.

"Seems rather understated," he said, proud that he didn't add *for you*.

"Yet perfectly on-brand for you."

Nolan's chest warmed in a way that startled him.

She was willingly toning things down, changing the story just enough so it would work for him. He wasn't used to that. In his family, he'd always been the black sheep, the one twisting himself to fit into his father's version of the perfect son.

Jess's willingness to compromise was more endearing than he expected. A small sign that she saw him beyond the overachieving persona he projected.

He looked down at the table, pleased they were finally on the same page. He nodded thoughtfully, liking the way this scenario sounded. "Okay, that works. A coffee proposal. But!" He held up a finger for emphasis. "Let's skip any long, drawn-out emotional stories, okay? Just the coffee proposal."

She cocked her head. "You want a romantic coffee proposal story sans feelings?"

"That is correct."

She studied him for a moment, then shook her head before taking the paper from his hand. Her fingers brushed against his, barely there, but it was enough to send a shock of electricity shooting up his arm. She wrote *proposal = hot coffee, no feelings* in the Anecdote column.

Then she looked up at him and flashed that charm-bomb of a smile and Nolan had to blink and wonder why the news hadn't mentioned there would be a solar eclipse that day.

"We're gonna crush this, Nolan. You'll see."

Before he could respond, she had slipped her hand into his, curling her fingers around him. He looked down at her hand and felt the weight of her, how her warmth heated his cool fingers.

Jess's fingers lingered just a fraction longer, brushing against his palm before she quickly pulled away. She looked down at her lap, cheeks flushed, and fiddled with her napkin, avoiding his gaze. Nolan's eyes followed her, his curiosity and concern piqued. *Why did she do that?* he wondered, unsettled by the brief glimpse of her vulnerability and unsure how to respond.

"It's a good story," Jess finished, a small smile tugging at her lips. "Simple and uncomplicated. Easy to keep under control."

She met his gaze briefly, then turned her attention back to her sushi, clearly signaling she was keeping her boundaries intact.

Nolan leaned back in his seat, slowly exhaling a measured breath. He wanted to say something—anything—that would bridge the distance he suddenly felt between them, but the words were all tangled up in his mind, and he knew they would refuse to come when he needed them.

Her retreat, polite but clear, left him feeling oddly hollow, aware of a subtle pull he couldn't name. He shook his head lightly to get back in the present moment. *Stay focused,* he told himself. *Stick to the plan.*

He smoothed his napkin before laying it next

to his empty plate. "I am in complete agreement. Keeping things simple is how we keep everything under control."

CHAPTER FOUR

"DR. HAYES!" YELLED THE EMS communications nurse. "Incoming helo. Ten minutes out!"

Jess's body went into overdrive as she mentally prepared for the arrival of a medical helicopter. "What do we know?"

The EMS communications nurse pressed a hand to her headset as she listened. "Patient is a male in his forties. High-speed collision. T-boned on the passenger side. Chest and belly pain. Heart rate 124, BP 102 over 80."

"Activate the trauma team and prep Trauma 1," Jess called.

The emergency department became a blur of bodies and sharp commands. The trauma team headed to the roof to meet the EMT team when they landed while the ED prepared for whatever their new patient would need.

Elevator doors opened with a ding, then a rush of bodies and voices headed her way. Jess caught a glimpse of a man moaning on the gurney. An attractive woman in her forties was by his side, her face lined with worry. She had blood on her face and chest, and was holding his hand.

"What's your name, sir?" the charge nurse called.

"James," the man said weakly.

Jess gave the man's shoulder a quick squeeze. "Hang in there, James. We've got you now." To her team, she yelled, "We're gonna need X-rays—chest and pelvis!"

"Got it!" someone called out.

The charge nurse intercepted the woman who appeared to be James's wife. "Ma'am, why don't you come with me and let the doctors do their job?"

The woman reluctantly let go of his hand. "I'll be right here, honey."

James tried to look up as she left, but his pain was too great. His head dropped back to the gurney with a moan.

"Move him to the ED bed on three: One, two, three."

"Should I start a femoral line?"

"I'll do that," called a nurse.

Jess checked the man's chest with her stethoscope. "His lungs are wet."

"The belly's soft but tender," said the charge nurse.

"Get a CBS, type and screen, KB and coags."

A half-dozen people buzzed about, an organized

chaos that Jess loved. At every moment, she knew she could count on her team to do the right thing.

Someone moved the X-ray machine over the bed. There was a whirring sound, then Jess was viewing an X-ray of James's lungs projected on a screen in the trauma space. One lung was nearly black while the other was clear and white.

"Left hemothorax—he's bleeding," Lena reported.

"Put in a chest tube and give him back all the blood you get out."

Another ED doctor quickly cleaned the side of the man's chest with Betadine, then numbed the area with lidocaine.

James whimpered from the stress and pain while his wife stood by the trauma bay entrance, looking helpless and overwhelmed.

"I'm in," the ED doctor called.

Relief flooded Jess's body. James was stabilized for the moment. "Secure the tube and let's get him over to CT."

Jess stayed with James while the attending radiologist completed the CAT scan.

"He has a contained rupture of the aorta, a pseudoaneurysm. It's leaking," Dr. Rourke, the attending radiologist, reported as they viewed the scan together.

"Okay, let's get him up to the cath lab, fix it."

"Can't do it," the radiologist said. "He has a severe anaphylactic reaction documented to iodinated contrast. He coded during a scan ten years ago. It's in the chart."

Jess's hope disappeared. The least invasive way to repair James's heart injury was TEVAR, a procedure where doctors could place a fabric-covered metal tube to reinforce the damaged artery and stop bleeding. It would help James avoid open heart surgery, but contrast was essential for fluoroscopic visualization during TEVAR. Without it, the surgeon would essentially be operating in the dark.

Rourke, still wearing the lead apron from the CT suite, waited for her input.

Jess swallowed hard. "So we're doing open repair."

"Yeah." Rourke nodded grimly. "Crack the chest, get control, repair the aorta the old-fashioned way. Higher risk, but it's the only viable option."

Jess nodded and the attending picked up the phone to alert the surgical team. James moaned, a ragged, broken sound. Jess put a hand on his shoulder.

"Sir," she said gently, leaning close, "we're going to take you to surgery right now. The surgeons are ready for you. We're doing everything we can."

His breathing hitched—fear or pain, she couldn't tell. "Can I see my wife first?"

"Blood pressure is dropping again," the trauma nurse called out. "Seventy systolic."

Jess knew time was of the essence. His situation could worsen at any moment, but how could she deny him such a simple request?

"Of course," she said. She alerted Lena to have his wife meet them back in the ED. Soon, she was at his side.

Jess motioned for the respiratory therapist to remove James's mask, then waved as many people as she could from the surgical bay to give James and his wife as much privacy as possible. But she had to stay to watch the monitors over his bed. Until he was wheeled into surgery, she couldn't leave him completely alone because of the critical nature of his condition.

"Honey, it will be okay, please don't be upset," he said in a soft and gentle voice. He raised his right hand and his wife folded it between her own. She struggled to smile through the tears that spilled despite her visible efforts to stay calm.

There was a long pause. So long that Jess glanced his way, and saw the angst in his eyes. She felt sure she knew he had words he wanted to say, but they did not come. Tears welled in her own eyes.

Tell her how much you love her, James.

Did he know how much danger he was in? That he was about to have open heart surgery, a risky procedure that could go either way with all the damage he had suffered?

Tell her! Jess whisper-screamed in her mind.

The man opened his mouth, then closed it. Then smiled at his wife and squeezed her hand. "The HVAC system needs to be tuned up this spring. Call Lucas & Sons. They have our information on file."

Jess couldn't imagine why James was worried about house repairs at a time like this, but his wife just gave him a gentle smile and an even gentler kiss.

"Everything will be okay," his wife assured him, and Jess desperately hoped she was right.

Then James told Jess his chest pain was increasing, and Jess knew they were out of time. The wife had to be shooed out of the room, the trauma team returned and then it was a blur of shouted orders and coordinated movements as they shuttled James from the emergency department to surgery.

Jess stared at the elevator doors once they had slid shut. James was out of her hands now. She had done her job stabilizing him as best she could—now it was up to the trauma team and the surgeons and the cardiologists to save his life. She gave his wife a quick update before sending her to the surgery floor to wait.

When Jess's twelve-hour shift finally ended a few hours later, she logged out of her last chart and reached for her bag just as the tracking board refreshed. Nolan's name flashed beside a new consult request, the timestamp fresh enough to mean he was already on his way down. For some reason, it made her hesitate and linger at her workstation a moment longer than necessary. She told herself it was nothing—just her habit of sticking around to see if she was needed. But there was a faint, unwelcome awareness coiling in her chest that said she was hoping their paths might cross again.

"Ugh," she muttered under her breath and only to herself. What was wrong with her?

Ever since their lunch date, things had felt different between them. He had seemed slightly less impatient during their consults, and she had felt slightly less dread at the prospect of seeing him again.

She hadn't been able to resist dragging him to a sushi restaurant and pelting him with outlandish suggestions for their engagement backstory. His reactions to her bizarre suggestions were just so...*serious.* How his nostrils had flared when she proposed a backstory where he was arrested for grand theft auto! It had taken every ounce of her self-control to not dissolve into a fit of laughter as he strained to remain professional and keep her on track.

What she *hadn't* counted on was looking up when he didn't expect it and catching his gaze trailing her leg. Or the slight tension in his shoulders when she had flipped her hair off her shoulder and leaned into his space.

If she didn't know better, she'd swear her colleague had been checking her out.

That possibility made it a lot harder to downplay the way her body reacted when he was around. He could hold her gaze in a way that made a shiver run down her spine. And when she had made up that story about his soulful brown eyes shattering her? Well, that wasn't entirely fiction.

The prospect that he might be attracted to her too had changed everything for her. She found herself drawn to his lean, disciplined body and the careful way he chose his words. Their lunch date had sparked a curiosity she hadn't expected. Nolan's attention had a different vibe than she had ever experienced. There were no games or hidden agendas, no charming lies like the ones Evan had spun.

The way Nolan stumbled through social and romantic cues made his interest feel more genuine and honest. And for the first time since they had forged their fake engagement, the Napa Valley weekend didn't feel like a chore. In fact, it might even be…fun.

Lena joined her in the locker room, looking as exhausted as Jess felt. Jess had been so busy for the rest of her shift, she never had a chance to ask how James had fared with his surgery.

Lena frowned when Jess asked her. "Sorry, Jess. He didn't make it."

Lena's words landed like a gut punch, and she didn't know why. She was a frequent witness to trauma and loss in the ED, but some cases slipped past her armor. James's certainly had. All she could think about was all those feelings she had seen in his eyes, and how James had missed his chance to put those feelings into words.

"Good night, Lena." Jess hoisted her gym bag over her shoulder and headed for the door. She had planned to stop by her gym on the way home and get in a workout while it was still dark and quiet. But the long, emotional night left her feeling wrung out. More interested in her bed and a good book than a heavy set of dumbbells.

"Bye, Jess."

Jess made her way down the hallway to the exit, already debating what she would have for breakfast. It was just a question of whether she had enough energy to make eggs, or if collapsing in bed with a bowl of cereal and cold milk was the best she could do.

She passed the elevator bank just as the stainless steel doors slid open. Nolan strode out, his long doctor's coat flapping as he rounded the corner and headed her way. Nolan seemed to have two speeds—slow and focused, or fast and focused. Never meandering.

He looked up from his computer tablet as she passed, his focused attention easing for a split second into something between recognition and a smile. The warmth of his expression caught her off guard, and she felt a flash of annoyance at herself for wanting to smile back.

"Jess," he said, as if she had been just the doctor he was looking for. "About the infant with the new-onset seizures—neurology agreed with your call. EEG was already lighting up."

"That's good," she said, slowing despite herself. "I'm glad they moved quickly." Her words were right, but she felt flat even as she delivered them. She was at the end of her emotional rope, and she just hoped Nolan didn't want to chat much longer.

Nolan hesitated before returning to his tablet. His gaze lingered a beat longer than necessary, flicking over her face instead of past it. "Is everything all right?"

"Fine," she replied automatically, adjusting the strap of her bag. She started to pivot away, eager to keep moving.

She made it a few steps down the hallway before she heard Nolan's footsteps.

"You don't look fine," he said, not unkindly. Just factual.

She stopped and turned to face him, shrugging her heavy gym bag off her shoulder to give her body a rest. "It's just been a long day with some tough cases."

He studied her gaze, then gestured down the hall. "Let's take a break. Follow me."

She opened her mouth to refuse, but something about his certainty felt comforting in her fatigue. She followed him to the physicians' lounge, leaving the hum of the ED behind them.

Nolan pulled out a chair and gestured for her to sit. He moved with purpose now, pouring coffee, setting it in front of her like he'd done this a million times before.

"Here," he said. "Drink."

She wrapped her hands around the cup, grateful despite herself. Nolan didn't press. He just pulled out a chair to sit across from her, his posture still rigidly formal, but he set his tablet aside to focus his attention on her.

"Whatever happened after our case," he said gently, "It doesn't look like nothing."

The concern in his voice—awkward, earnest, unmistakably real—caught her off guard. Of all the ways Nolan had surprised her as of late, the look in his eyes was the most surprising twist of all.

She sighed. "I lost a patient this afternoon. Male in his forties with a damaged aorta after a car wreck. He wasn't eligible for TEVAR, so we sent him to surgery." She looked away, her mind full of James's story. He still had so much life ahead of him. "I really thought he'd make it."

"That's tough. You okay?"

Was she okay? When was the last time anyone had asked her that? Evan would have given her a pat on the shoulder by now, then some canned platitudes before rushing off. He would have been charming as hell to distract her, but in the end, she would have felt dismissed and unimportant.

Nolan wasn't rushing anywhere. His dark brown eyes were studying her with a small head tilt that made her feel really seen.

It was unnerving, really. But also really nice.

She smoothed the wrinkles in her scrub pants with the palms of her hands. "Just another day in the ED, right?"

"But this patient was different?"

She bit her lip, remembering how James had looked at his wife, his eyes full of unspoken words.

Jess sighed and decided to just spill it. "He asked if he could see his wife before we took him to surgery. I think he knew he was in danger. I gave him as much space as I could, but…he never said he loved her. I think he really wanted to, but he didn't. Instead, he told her that their HVAC needed fixing." Anguish replaced her angst. "Why the hell wouldn't he use that time to tell her he loved her? He knew how sick he was."

She looked up at Nolan as if he might really have the answers. But his expression remained calm, carefully neutral.

"Maybe that was how he did tell her he loved her," Nolan said. "By taking care of details like that."

The idea caught Jess off guard. She'd never thought of love expressed sideways, through action instead of language. It felt uncomfortably plausible, and yet, perfectly on point that Nolan saw it so easily.

"Maybe," she said.

His explanation should have soothed her. But it did little to calm the feelings that were swirling in her chest.

"He kind of reminded me of my dad. He had similar facial features."

"And that's why this upset you? Because you fear your dad could die too?"

She flicked her hair away from her face, wishing she had a hair tie to keep everything under control. "No, I think it was more that he'd die with unfinished business."

Nolan waited while she struggled to make sense of the blizzard of emotions making her muscles tight.

"My dad has trouble speaking his mind too. I guess I just hope…"

He waited while the truth bubbled up from the depths of her heart. She had been avoiding dealing with her greatest fear for so long. That she had perhaps hastened her father's demise by taking him away from everything he loved. And that maybe she had broken his heart—for good.

Nolan's patient body language and concerned expression were too much right now. She and Nolan might be on friendlier terms, but there was no way she was about to reveal her deepest fear and regret to him. They weren't even friends—not really. Just two colleagues in a very strange situation.

She took a deep breath and got back in her emotional lane. “Anyway! James just reminded me of my father, that’s all. I guess that’s what rattled me.”

She drank the last of the coffee that Nolan had made for her, then went to the sink to rinse and dry the mug. When she turned back around, Nolan hadn’t moved.

He was watching her with a faint crease between his brows, his usual, easy confidence stripped away. His hands were splayed on the table, as if bracing himself for stability. For a man so sure of his abilities, he suddenly looked uncertain, almost wrong-footed.

Jess recognized the look immediately. It was the expression of someone replaying the last few minutes, searching for the misstep. She’d felt that way plenty of times herself, when Evan had suddenly changed their plans or shut down a personal conversation lest he reveal too much about himself.

Those rejections always left her feeling like she had done something wrong, but could never figure out what it was, or how to make things right.

What unsettled her was that Nolan didn’t look closed off at all. He looked concerned…about her. Almost like he feared he had failed her somehow. The realization did not match up with the assumptions she had carried since she met him six months earlier, when he joined the staff of Horizon Bay. That he was all precision and ambition, more machine than man and engineered to achieve and not much more.

But machines didn't make coffee for tired colleagues.

The realization that she had been wrong about him tugged at her. She didn't want to leave Nolan feeling she had shut him out of her personal life. But how to make things right with a man who avoided sentimentality as if was a contagious disease?

"Hey," she said. "You owe me a favor, don't you?"

His shoulders eased a fraction, but the crease between his brows persisted.

"My father? Remember? I'm not the only one who has to figure out how to pass for a fiancée."

His attention sharpened. "That's right. We had an agreement."

She exhaled a little sigh of relief. Nolan was back in his lane, focused on agreements and how to fulfill them.

"He called again this morning. He's excited to meet you."

"When were you thinking?" Nolan asked.

"Would Saturday afternoon work? We could have lunch at his facility, or maybe take him out if he's feeling strong enough."

Nolan checked his calendar app. "That works."

Relief loosened something in her chest. "Thank you. Really."

As they headed for the door, Jess couldn't help noticing something unsaid humming between them. It felt like they had their own unfinished business, but she couldn't imagine what.

Nolan stood in the center of his bedroom, sunlight casting clean lines across the hardwood floors. He surveyed his wardrobe options with the same methodical calm he brought to a pre-op briefing. His town house was immaculate, as usual, with clutter kept to a minimum and everything tidied by his weekly housekeeping service. He wasn't a germophobe per se, but he found order to be a calming counterpoint to his demanding life as a doctor.

Jess had given him a few clues about how to make the best impression on her father. *Strive for respectful, but be approachable. Don't wear a suit, but nothing too casual either. Look like you're taking this seriously, but not like you're trying too hard.*

He ran his hand over the neatly folded shirts he had stacked on his bed. He loved a good challenge, and Jess's contradictory instructions amused him. If there was a way to make the right impression on her father, he would figure it out. He had plenty of experience trying to please his own father that would hopefully help him connect with hers.

He settled on a soft blue button-down that she had once complimented in passing. It had not escaped his notice which of his shirts made her nod in approval, and which simply made her gaze slide away. He hadn't thought about it at the time, the way he noted her reactions to him or memorized how she took her coffee. He told himself that's just how he was. A guy who gathered data wherever he went, and he genuinely believed that she was just part of the data set that was Horizon Bay.

But the truth was, it was because he had studied her that he recognized her distress that night in the hospital hallway. And then it wasn't so easy to pretend the information he liked to squirrel away had been neutral. Somewhere along the path of working together, he'd taken an interest in her.

His cell phone buzzed. He checked his phone. It was a text message from Jess.

My Dad's rehab facility is closer to you. Should I just meet you there?

Nolan paused to consider her question. It would be most practical for them to meet at her father's place. But some new part of him rebelled. This new part was a stranger to him, thinking about things that were not practical, yet pleased him greatly. Like the chance to spend a little more time with Jess.

Engaged couples usually show up together.

Nolan finished dressing, settling on dark jeans that he pressed to a crisp line but were softened by wear. He paired them with the pale blue button-down, the sleeves unbuttoned and rolled just once for a casual effect. Hopefully he looked like a man who respected the occasion of meeting his fiancée's father.

As he drove across town to her apartment, his thoughts drifted back to the break room. It had been a big risk, reaching out to her like that, to see if she wanted to talk about whatever was clearly bothering her. It wasn't his modus operandi at all, but he couldn't ignore how exhausted she looked when they crossed paths. And how upset.

He could see it in the circles under her eyes, the droop in her shoulders. Something unfamiliar had stirred in him that felt protective and nurturing. He couldn't just let her go home like that. Not without at least providing a fortifying cup of coffee.

But while she might have appreciated his clumsy efforts at comfort, she didn't trust him enough to share whatever was really bothering her.

But she had made her feelings clear. Hunched over her coffee, she had softly and sweetly turned him down. Her rejection was delivered with an easy smile to soften the blow, but still, it had stirred an old familiar ache deep in his chest. Once again, he was on the outside looking in. Tolerated but not welcome, just as it had always been with his family.

He tried to ignore the sting and be logical about it all. Why should she trust him with something personal? They were just colleagues, after all, who had clashed for months over details big and small.

Still, old familiar doubts pressed at him. Had he misread her? Wanted more than what was offered? He wasn't sure. He just knew that they were in a strange limbo now. More than colleagues, not quite friends, and still figuring out what their boundaries were outside of work.

All that mattered now was getting through his part of their arrangement. She had asked him to spend one afternoon posing as her fiancé. He could do that.

When Jess opened her apartment door, Nolan's first thought was that she looked beautiful.

His second was that something was wrong.

She usually greeted the world in color—bold skirts, playful prints, jewelry that caught the light when she laughed. Today she wore soft neutrals instead. A simple dress with minimal makeup and her hair pulled back into a tidy bun. She looked as if she had smoothed away anything that might draw too much attention.

This wasn't the Jess he knew.

"Wow," he said, because the word escaped before he could stop it. "You look…really beautiful."

A flicker of surprise crossed her face, quickly replaced by that familiar, sunny smile. "Thanks. Ready?"

He nodded, though his gaze lingered a beat too long. This version of Jess felt strategic somehow.

Something told him that this meeting with her father was going to be different.

The drive across the city was too quiet, making him aware of the tension humming between them. This seemed like a good time to do some reconnaissance work.

He asked lightly, “So, what kind of fiancé would Jess Hayes bring home to Dad?” He wasn’t sure if she would remember a throwback to her taunt in his office, when he had first proposed the ruse.

She shifted her focus from the landscape outside her window to him. “Oh wow. Putting me on the spot?”

“Seems only fair,” he said. “You grilled me.”

She tilted her head, thinking. “I’m not really sure what kind of man he’s expecting.”

“Oh, come on. He must have had some reactions to the boys you brought home in high school?”

She looked out the window. “Not really. Nothing I can recall, anyway.”

That struck Nolan as odd. He knew from their talks that her father was a salt of the earth type, a farmer who worked the same plot of land his father and grandfather before him had worked. It seemed strange that her father would take little interest in his only daughter’s social life.

“My dad didn’t really get *involved* with my life, you know? He had a lot of work to do. Farming is a sunup to sundown kind of life. Then the evenings are for taking care of the animals, repairing equipment, and going to sleep until it's time to start again."

"But he had help, right?"

"He had me," she said with a smile. "And migrant workers he hired to help with the harvest. But no, otherwise, it was just us."

Nolan knew a little about farming life. His father had bought their Napa Valley vineyard after a short but lucrative career in professional football. He thought it would be good for his boys to grow their "football muscles," and he wanted them to learn the value of a long day of hard work.

He and his brother had both worked the land alongside their father, but they had also had a full roster of employees to help.

"So what kind of fiancé would he expect?"

"A hard worker. That's a must. Who maybe loves farming or at least something hands-on. Maybe a reader. My dad loves to read."

"And someone who's good to you?" he prompted.

Jess looked up, a little surprised. "Oh sure, of course."

They pulled into the driveway of the rehab facility. Jess squared her shoulders and pulled down the mirror to freshen her lipstick.

Inside, her father was already waiting in the lobby—a tall, silver-haired man with a flat, assessing stare that was the exact opposite of Jess's sunshine. Nolan felt Jess go tense beside him, then she burst into a flurry of cheerful banter.

They settled at the small wrought iron table at the center of the garden, roses climbing the fence in careful, disciplined rows. Jess moved here and there, brisk and efficient, laying out the coffee and croissants she had brought from home.

"Cream?" she asked her father. He nodded and she adjusted his coffee just so before setting it before him.

Nolan watched with interest as the Jess he knew became someone else. The Jess he knew from work was relaxed and confident. Always ready with a retort or a joke. This version of Jess was hyperattentive, intent on meeting her father's needs before he asked. She hovered, half standing, half sitting, her attention fixed on him in a way that made Nolan's chest tighten.

At the hospital she was kinetic, all quick smiles and easy confidence, her voice warm even when she was delivering hard truths. Around her father, she was…careful. Her shoulders were drawn back too straight, her movements deliberate, as if she were bracing for inspection.

Her father barely noticed.

"So," he said, turning his genial weathered face toward Nolan. "Tell me a little about yourself."

"I'm a pediatric hospitalist at Horizon Bay," Nolan said. "That's where I met your daughter. We work together on a lot of cases."

Her father nodded, smiling with vague approval, then frowned slightly, as if something didn't quite line up. "Wasn't the last fellah you dated a doctor too?" he asked Jess.

The shift in her was immediate. Her smile held, but it tightened, like a knot pulled too fast. "Yeah," she said lightly. "But that was a long time ago."

"Same hospital?"

"Yes," she said, just as lightly. "But different departments."

The answer seemed to satisfy him. Or perhaps it simply didn't matter enough to pursue. He leaned back in his chair and launched into a story about the farm, about long days and longer nights, about the years he'd put in working the land mostly on his own.

Nolan listened, nodding in the right places, but his attention snagged on the word *alone*.

"But Jess helped, right?" He already knew the answer because they had discussed it on the drive over. About summers that began before sunrise and ended with sore muscles and dirt ground into her palms.

Her father paused to consider Nolan's question. "Jess?" he repeated, as if surprised by the name. "Oh. Yeah. I guess she helped a little here and there."

Nolan glanced sideways at Jess.

She was smiling again, wide and generous, offering a joke Nolan suspected she'd rehearsed a thousand times. Her father didn't quite hear it. Or maybe he did and didn't register that it mattered. The words drifted past him like background noise.

In that moment, Nolan could see the truth, all at once and undeniable. He had misjudged Jess. Or maybe not seen her at all. She wasn't Miss Sunshine-and-Moonbeams as he had labeled her months ago. Not for real anyway. All that brightness was her armor. A way to pretend she was so happy, no one had to notice or tend to her sadness or pain.

Jess's father might love her, but she was an afterthought in his story.

Nolan felt a familiar ache settle low in his chest. He'd grown up on a vineyard. He knew what it took to bring crops to market, how no harvest came together without hands willing to bleed for it. And from Jess's stories, he knew she'd been one of those hands. If her father couldn't remember that, what else had slipped past him?

Had there been times she needed his help and protection, but he wasn't around? Had she ever been hurt and had to stuff it away, because there was no one around to care?

Jess sat beside Nolan now, close enough that he could see her profile clearly. Her posture was still, guarded. The smile she wore was flawless. A few weeks ago, he would have believed this was Jess, always in a good mood no matter what happened around her.

But now he saw the truth. The real Jess lived

somewhere behind that smile and the snark she wielded so deftly at work.

Nolan watched her for another beat, something steady and unfamiliar taking root inside him.

He was starting to think he'd like to meet that version of Jess Hayes.

CHAPTER FIVE

NOLAN TRAILED JESS through the men's section of the department store.

"I hope I'm not about to regret my life choices," he said. "Will there be any boundaries on the shirt selections today?"

Jess paused just long enough to smile and respond. "No ruffles. I promise. Besides, this is on you. I offered to let you off the hook for shirt shopping, remember?"

Nolan craned his neck to get a look at the shirts she was considering.

"Well, I think it makes sense."

"Really? How so?" She half listened as she combed through the orderly racks of menswear.

He nodded. "Your wardrobe is, shall we say, eclectic."

"I'm going to take that as a compliment, Nolan."

The hint of a smile tugged at his mouth. "Just wanted to make sure we don't clash."

"Like we do at the hospital?"

"Exactly. Plus, it's more practice for the wedding, right?"

She chuckled as she pulled several shirts from the rack, holding them up against his chest with a stylist's eye. Crisp whites and pale blues first. These were safe choices—very Nolan. Then she added a few others. A soft chambray with subtle texture. A pale gray with a faint blue undertone.

"These are a little outside your norm," she warned lightly. "But I think they could work."

"You know my norm?" he asked, his interest clearly piqued.

"The whole hospital knows your norms, Nolan. Now go."

She sent him off to the dressing room with an armful of hangers and wandered toward the tie display, grateful for the distance. Silk ties fanned out like paint swatches, orderly and restrained. She touched one, then another, her mind drifting despite herself.

The visit with her father rose up, uninvited.

Nolan had been the perfect fiancé. He had been attentive to her father, asked good questions, and laughed at all the right times.

But what had surprised her—what she hadn't asked for—was how he had been there for *her*. He noticed when she went quiet because her father's attention had slid away from her yet again.

It had surprised her. And pleased her more than she cared to admit.

That visit with her father was supposed to help her father stay motivated to keep up with his exercise. But it had become a lot more than that. Nolan had managed to draw her attention to something she had spent most of her life ignoring. How her father overlooked her sometimes, and took her for granted.

She knew her dad loved her, but that knowledge lived in her brain, not her heart. She had never felt truly seen by her father, and certainly never felt him step up to make sure she was included or protected. Not like Nolan had done in the short time they had known each other.

The realization had followed her into darker territory. Was that why she'd accepted Evan's limited affection for so long? Because it felt familiar? Because she was used to being overlooked, and that felt safer than risking wanting more?

She considered a navy tie, then put it back.

But nothing had surprised her more than when Nolan had taken her hand under the table. Not squeezed it. Just placed it on his thigh and folded his own hand over it, warm and steady.

She'd looked up at him, startled.

Was this part of the ruse?

He'd glanced at her sideways, a gentle smile in his eyes. No, this wasn't for her father's benefit. It was just for her.

I've got you, Jess.

It had been the best visit she'd ever had with her

dad. He'd told his stories, all of them, and she'd sat there feeling, for once, that someone at the table truly cared that she was there.

She selected a few ties and draped them over her arm, then drifted to the next display.

How many days till the wedding? She mentally calculated—just one more week.

And then what?

Would everything go back to how it was before? She and Nolan retreating to their respective floors at the hospital, reduced to consults and chance encounters in elevators?

There was a new, fledgling connection between them that she didn't want to lose. That thought gnawed at her in a way she didn't want to examine too closely.

Nolan was growing on her. Worse, he was revealing himself to be exactly the kind of man she'd always told herself not to want. Beneath that grumpy, rigid exterior was a kind, observant man who noticed what people needed and quietly provided it.

"Jess?"

She turned to find him standing there, one shirt already on, another draped over his arm. In his hand was one of the stretch options.

"What do you think?" he asked.

She tilted her head, appraising him. "I like it."

The shirt was a soft slate blue, lighter than his usual palette, with a subtle texture that caught the light. It softened him somehow, made him look more approachable and friendly.

"Oh, hold on," she said suddenly. "I've got the perfect tie for that."

She shuffled through the ties she'd selected, then pulled out the one she'd hidden beneath the others. Baby blue silk scattered with hot pink flamingos.

"What do you think?"

He arched an eyebrow. He didn't fall for her pranks as easily now.

"I'll bet you thought this was exactly what I'd choose for you," she teased.

"You're absolutely right," he said. "Actually," he rummaged through the ties draped over her arm. "I think this one is perfect."

"Let's see if you're right."

Without thinking, she stepped forward into his space and flipped up the collar of his shirt.

Then she realized how close she was. Mere inches from his chest. Close enough to detect his mint-scented breath and feel the contours of a body he had shaped through years of martial arts.

He stood tall and utterly still, his gaze scanning her face. But where she had once found his intense gaze intimidating, it now just felt electrifying.

A shiver traced her spine.

His eyes were brown. Deep, warm, flecked with gold. How had she not noticed the gold before? And his cologne smelled like clean linen and ocean air. Sharp and refreshing.

She gave him a quick, nervous smile. "Sorry. I didn't mean to…"

But she was here now.

She looped the tie around his neck, the silk cool against her fingers. She focused on the pattern as she worked, the familiar rhythm of crossing and flipping, though her hands felt anything but steady.

It took just a few seconds, but it felt like an hour.

She slid the knot up to his collar and smoothed it into place. "There," she said softly. "What do you think?"

She motioned for him to turn toward the mirror.

Instead, his gaze lingered on her face for one last, charged second. There was something in the way he looked at her that felt almost provocative, but that could not be right.

She stepped back, abruptly aware of where they were. Who they were.

This was still Nolan. They were on friendlier terms now, but he was still a colleague.

She had sworn she'd never date within the hospital again. It was too risky to her reputation.

And even if they weren't colleagues, they were just too different. She didn't want to have to work for affection again. She wanted romance, and love, and never, ever wondering where she stood with her lover.

Nolan was a good man; she had no doubt about that. But he was also the same man who couldn't come up with a romantic backstory for their fake engagement to save his life.

Nolan was stability and data and predictability. She wanted more, and after what happened with Evan, she would never settle for half of someone's heart ever again.

He turned away at last, almost reluctantly, and adjusted the tie. She bit her bottom lip as she watched. He really was a handsome man. She could see why her colleagues had called him The Professor. He had a stately, formal air about him that made her want to mess up his hair, just to see what he would do.

They left the store together with the garment bag draped over his arm. Outside the department store, a coffee cart promised every variation of hot and cold coffee drinks known to mankind. Nolan ordered an Americano with room for milk while she splurged on an oat milk latte with cinnamon.

They walked slowly toward his car, mindlessly discussing hospital cases and city news. As they approached his Audi, Jess had a surprising realization. She was a little bummed that their morning was coming to an end.

Their shopping trip had been, well, fun. If someone would have told her a month ago that she would even be shopping with Nolan, let alone enjoying it, she would have thought they were just plain crazy.

He opened the passenger door for her, then slid

behind the wheel and set the GPS for her apartment. Instead of the fastest route, he selected the back roads, letting the car glide through quieter streets.

At a stoplight, he glanced over. "Want to pick the music?"

"I'm permitted to touch your imperial time machine?" she asked in mock awe.

A corner of his mouth lifted. He tapped the display on the console, navigating with practiced ease. "There. Whatever you want."

She scrolled past categories. Classic. Hard rock. Heavy metal. Then she stopped, surprised by a familiar title she had not heard in years.

The cabin filled with the sound of acoustic guitars and brushed drums.

The sound tugged something loose in her chest. It brought her back to college, to feeling homesick for the Minnesota farm she had grown up on, while also beginning to find her footing in the world. Becoming someone new without fully understanding who that might be yet.

Her thoughts were interrupted by a low hum.

She turned to discover that Nolan was singing along.

"You know this song?" she asked.

"What?" He glanced at her briefly, still watching the road.

"This is 'Passenger Side' by Harbor & Pine. You know them?"

"Sure do." His hands crossed smoothly over each other as he made a turn. "Saw them in Detroit."

"No way. I saw them there too."

He looked at her with arched eyebrows. "What year?"

She told him. "I used to have the album from that live performance, but I must have lost it when I moved here."

He shook his head, a slow smile spreading. "Imagine that. Same venue. Same time. Yet we didn't meet for another decade and on the opposite side of the country. Some people might call that fate."

"Fate?" She laughed. "No way. That's way too woo-woo for Dr. Nolan Stone."

"You are absolutely right," he said, smiling.

The chorus rose again, and this time they sang together, softly at first, then a little more confidently.

"We were broke but breathing in borrowed light,
Maps folded wrong, still we swore we were right.
You said, 'I'll drive if you promise to stay,'
So I took the passenger side—hey hey."

Nolan kept an eye on the road, his posture relaxed and easy, one hand draped over the steering wheel.

It wasn't hard to imagine him in college, fresh-faced and hopeful, ready to take on the world.

What had young Nolan hoped for back then? Was he happy with how things had turned out?

Was she?

Nolan turned into her apartment complex and navigated to her building, pulling smoothly into a parking spot before shifting into Park.

"I can walk you up," he offered.

She felt a strange spark of anticipation, sharp and electric. She knew she should say no. It was only a few flights of stairs, and she didn't have much to carry.

"Yes," she heard herself say.

They climbed the stairs together and stopped outside her door.

"Thanks for helping with the shirt," Nolan said.

"Sure."

"And for not making me wear the pink flamingo tie."

She smiled. "Well, we do have to work together after the wedding."

She hesitated, keys cool and heavy in her hand. Nolan stood close enough that she could hear each breath he took. If she leaned back even slightly, she would be pressed against him.

She paused for a moment, then turned the key in the lock and opened the door. For some reason, moving away from him felt like breaking some kind of magnetic pull.

"Well," he said finally, his voice lower than usual. "This was…nice."

Nolan's usual habit of understating things made her smile. She took a moment to really study him before he looked up. The afternoon sun softened his features and made him look less guarded.

"I had fun too," she said.

Time stood suspended for a long moment as neither of them moved away. His gaze dropped briefly to her mouth, and Jess felt her pulse quicken in response.

Just then, her neighbor's door swung open.

"Oh! Sorry. Excuse me." Mrs. Kline bustled out, terrier tugging eagerly at the leash, nails clicking against the floor.

"Well, hello there, young man," Mrs. Kline said brightly, not bothering to hide her interest as she passed.

"Afternoon," Nolan replied smoothly, stepping aside.

The dog paused to sniff Nolan's shoe before being tugged along. A charged silence filled the space between them, punctuated by the ordinary hallway sounds of apartment life.

When they were alone again, Jess laughed softly. "Well. Timing is everything."

"It is," Nolan said, his smile careful now.

Jess felt an odd mix of relief and disappointment at her neighbor's interruption. Some current had started to pulse between them, making her wonder what she might have done had her neighbor not chosen that moment to walk her dog.

Jess tucked a snippet of hair behind her ear. "Bye, Nolan."

Nolan nodded. "Bye, Jess."

Jess walked confidently across her threshold and closed the door. Then she braced her back against it and closed her eyes. Her heart was still racing at how he had studied her lips.

Something was slowly shifting between them, and it made her feel unsteady and off balance. It was getting harder to believe their practice for the wedding was strictly make-believe.

"Jess! They need you in there—stat!"

Lena's urgent tone made the hairs on the back of her neck stand up. Before Jess could ask what was wrong, the door to Room 3, the ED's major resuscitation room, swung open. One of the nurses stepped out and yelled to Lena. "Page for any general surgeon to come to the emergency room!" Then she disappeared back into the room.

Paging any available surgeon was extremely unusual. It usually meant that whoever was in Room 3 was in imminent danger of dying.

Jess broke into a run, pushing through the door to find an impressive team already assembled. Several nurses. Her boss. An ENT. Nolan. All of them crowded around a gurney.

Lena filled her in as she dialed another number. "We've got a little kid who's not breathing. I'm calling everyone I can."

Jess's stomach clenched. If they were calling for any surgeon at all, there was a good chance they were heading toward a tracheotomy—an emergency airway cut straight into the neck. On a toddler, it was a nightmare scenario.

She took in the room in a single, sharp sweep. Nolan was bent over the head of the bed, laryngoscope in hand, working the instrument into the child's mouth. A respiratory therapist hovered with suction ready. Two nurses searched desperately for veins. Two paramedics pressed against the wall, sweat-soaked and shaken.

"IV in place!" a nurse called.

"I've still got a pulse, but it's slowing," Lena said, fingers at the child's wrist as she watched the monitor.

Nolan swore and pulled the laryngoscope free. "Can't get it," he said sharply. The respiratory therapist immediately began bagging the child, forcing oxygen into lungs that resisted every squeeze.

"What do we have?" Jess asked, already tugging on gloves.

"Eighteen-month-old," Lena said. "Mom saw her choking. Doesn't know on what. She stopped breathing before EMS arrived."

Jess moved closer, her chest tightening at the sight of the tiny body on the stretcher. Her patient was a little girl wearing a fairy costume and purple glitter shoes. An ordinary morning, abruptly broken.

She pressed her stethoscope to the girl's chest. "Is she hard to bag?"

"Very," the therapist said.

Nolan's gaze snapped to Jess. "There's something obstructing her airway. I can't see past it, and I can't visualize the cords." Sweat slicked his forehead now, darkening his scrubs. "If we don't establish an airway, she's not going to make it."

Jess swallowed hard. "Give me the scope."

Nolan hesitated, then shook his head. "Protocol says after a failed intubation, we move to a surgical airway."

Her pulse kicked. "On an eighteen-month-old?" she shot back. "Her trachea is the size of a straw. You cut her neck, you risk collapsing it entirely."

"Jess," he said, tight and controlled, "I know you like to think big picture, but right now, we don't have the luxury of perfect options."

"That doesn't mean we have to kill her with the wrong one," she countered. "A trach on a child this small, in this chaos? You know the complication rate."

Dr. Wilson glanced between them. "You think you can get the tube in?"

Jess didn't hesitate. "Yes."

Nolan stared at her, conflict plain on his face. He wanted the certainty that came with following the rules, not for his own sake, but for the girl's.

But Jess knew there was nothing sure at this moment. They could do everything right and still lose this baby.

"She's blue," he said. "We're running out of time."

"I know," Jess said fiercely. "But if we cut her, we can't undo it. Let me try."

The room seemed to hold its breath.

Nolan closed his eyes for a brief second. When he opened them, his voice was steady but strained. "One attempt. If you can't visualize, we do the trach."

Jess nodded. "One attempt."

He handed her the laryngoscope.

She dropped to her knees at the head of the bed, angling herself for the best possible view. The blade slid into the child's mouth, the small light illuminating a landscape of pink-red tissue that refused to make sense.

She suctioned. Repositioned. Looked again.

Nothing.

Her heart hammered. She pulled back so the respiratory therapist could oxygenate again. Jess's hands were trembling just enough that she noticed.

She looked down at the child's face. Long hair. Thick lashes. Lying far too still for a toddler.

Something wasn't right. There were landmarks she ought to be able to see that would guide the blade past her tongue and into her airway. But her anatomy was distorted so that all Jess saw was swollen red tissue everywhere. Not just swelling though—something different.

Think, dammit!

Was this some sort of congenital anomaly? She had never seen anything like it.

Jess waved the therapist closer. She reinserted the blade, this time angling deeper, further back than instinct said she should, toward the esophagus instead of away from it. If this was her last chance to save this girl before cutting her, she was going to do it.

She lifted the blade. And then she saw it.

A red blur surged upward beneath the blade, fast and violent, straight toward her face.

Time slowed as the object shot free, clearing the child's mouth and sailing into the air. It landed on the stretcher, bounced once, then rolled across the floor until it came to rest against the wall.

A red rubber ball.

For one suspended heartbeat, no one moved. Then the child cried, a full-throated indignant wail.

Color rushed back into the little girl's cheeks. Her limbs jerked and kicked. Only then did Jess sag back on her heels, exhaling a giant breath of relief.

Nolan caught her gaze, his expression unreadable.

Her chest warmed, the familiar rush of relief flooding her veins. There was no feeling like it—

knowing a child would live because she and her team had saved them.

Someone retrieved the ball, cleaned it, and handed it to her. The perfect choking hazard. Small enough to swallow. Large enough to lodge deep and distort the airway beyond recognition.

After the room settled, the girl was reunited with her sobbing mother. Jess wrote orders for overnight observation, but she felt confident that the worst was behind them.

The team dispersed, and Jess was called to another pediatric case. She lost track of Nolan until he found her an hour later in one of the empty consultation rooms off the pediatrics wing.

Jess had scrubbed her hands twice and still felt the phantom pressure of the laryngoscope in her grip. She was staring at the wall-mounted monitor without really seeing it when he knocked once and stepped inside.

"Got a minute?" he asked.

She nodded. "Sure."

He closed the door behind him, making the room feel smaller instantly.

"I wanted to review the case. Specifically, what you saw."

Jess felt her muscles tense up at Nolan's clinical words and careful tone. This was the Nolan she had always known. Eager to call out her mistakes or lecture her on some detail he thought she had missed. She couldn't believe he was doing this now, and on such a difficult case.

Jess folded her arms, bracing herself for worst. "What? You think I got lucky?"

"No." He shook his head quickly. "I think you saw something I didn't."

That made her stop in her tracks. What was Nolan saying here? That she had been right?

He dragged a chair closer to her, its metal legs screeching on the linoleum. He sat down next to her and leaned closer, so his eyes met hers. "When you said you wanted to try again, even after two failed laryngoscope attempts, you were sure. Why?"

Jess let out a breath. "Because her anatomy didn't make sense," she said. "I thought I was seeing swelling everywhere, but still, I should have been able to sight her tonsils or other landmarks. It was some kind of weird displacement that was pushing everything out of the way."

Nolan listened closely, but his expression didn't seem judgmental. His entire vibe was earnest, eager to hear what she would say next.

"But you were ready to cut," she said quietly. She tried not to make it sound like an accusation.

His jaw tightened. "Hell, yes. If you weren't in that room, I probably would have done it."

His response surprised her with his honesty and directness. He was admitting that he would have chosen the higher risk procedure because he didn't believe anything else was possible.

"I'm not sorry I pushed back," she said. "I would do it again."

"You shouldn't be sorry. Because you were right. I was wrong."

There were no signs of The Professor now. Nolan's usual demeanor of total competence and control had slipped, revealing a man who looked a little shaken. Like he had lost faith in something he had believed in very much, and didn't know what to do next.

"I would have followed protocol," he said in a tone that felt like confession. "They're reliable. They don't let you down."

Jess swallowed. "People do," she said before she could stop herself. She meant it as an expression of camaraderie, but it sounded more like a confession.

His gaze lifted to hers, then tilted his head.

"Evan," he said quietly.

Damn, she had revealed too much.

"I imagine you've heard all about that," she said, looking down at her nails. "I certainly have."

He shrugged. "A little."

"He was the biggest mistake I never knew I was making. I thought I was just the best girlfriend ever, so understanding when he canceled plans or showed up late. Of course, he was hiding the huge secret of being married. But I didn't know that. He just made me feel like I was asking for too much."

Nolan's hands clenched on the tabletop.

"He was wrong to lie to you," Nolan said.

"Yes, but I was wrong to let him treat me like an afterthought." Jess let out a breath that shook more than she wanted it to. "I needed you to listen to me back there," she admitted. "Not because I wanted to be right. But I need to be able to trust that you'll have my back when it matters."

"I do have your back," Nolan said. "That's why I stopped."

"But you didn't want to," she said.

"No," he said honestly. "I don't like leaps of faith." He hesitated. "But I've seen you save lives by trusting your instincts. I just—"

"You just don't trust yours," she finished softly.

Silence stretched between them, thick with tension.

"I spent my whole life in a house where winning was the only proof you belonged," he said. "I wasn't built to win like them. I excel in spaces where discipline and focus count for a lot."

Jess's chest tightened. "But today," she said, "rules would've hurt her."

"I know."

It hit her then—how much trust it took for him to step outside the rules that had always kept him safe, to choose *her* judgment on such a high-stakes case. Nolan didn't just see her in a way that the men in her life had missed. He had trusted her. He had put himself in the incredibly vulnerable position of believing he was right, yet trusting her anyway.

And in the quiet aftermath of that realization, another truth surfaced—one she hadn't been ready to think about until now. She was starting to trust Nolan too, in a way that felt new and unsettling. If he had insisted on following protocol tonight, she wouldn't have assumed he was being overly rigid. She would have believed he was acting in good faith, protecting their patient in ways he knew best. She would have stopped to reassess her own impulses, wondering if he might see something she was missing.

Something subtle shifted between them. She told herself it was because they were becoming a team. That they were starting to understand and respect how the other thought.

But he had taken a step closer without seeming to realize it. Or maybe he did. Something was shifting in his expression that looked like his guard was slipping.

"I don't know how to do things halfway," he said quietly. "Trust. Or...anything."

He was close enough now for their breaths to tangle. The space between them buzzed with electric anticipation, like the moment just before a summer storm breaks.

She knew they weren't talking about their emergency case anymore. They were talking about this strange pull between them that she had felt ever since they met. She had been able to keep it at bay by leaning into their friction and disagreements at work. But pretending to be his fiancée had opened new windows into the man behind the perfectly pressed white coat and meticulously organized office.

A slow, unmistakable warmth spread through her chest, down her arms, into the soft, wanting places she'd taught herself to ignore. Every nerve in her body was quietly retuning itself to Nolan's presence. It felt like she was standing too close to an open flame—pleasant at first, almost comforting—until the heat sharpened and she realized she was leaning in without meaning to. By the time her brain finally sounded the alarm, her heart had already stepped forward, curious and unafraid. The world narrowed to the space between them. She could smell the antiseptic bite of the hospital disinfectant clinging to his clothes, and beneath that, a faint trace of pure Nolan. Her pulse was loud in her ears as his breath grazed her cheek. If she moved even an inch closer, there would be no pretending that this was just practice.

"Nolan," she said, barely more than a whisper. Something was happening to her that didn't feel careful or planned.

Nolan closed the last inch between them, choosing her over what they both knew they ought to do. For a single, breathless moment, the warmth of him felt like gravity itself—steady, anchoring, unmistakably right. Then his mouth was on hers, warm and searching. His kiss, soft and deliberate, made her chest ache with longing. She tasted coffee and something clean and familiar, and the way his hand found her waist made her feel solidly grounded with him. The kiss didn't rush or linger, but it held, as if they were both memorizing the shape of it. When he drew back, her breath came uneven, her skin burning where he'd touched her. She knew, with a clarity that startled her, that he hadn't planned that kiss.

She pressed her fingers to her still-warm lips and felt a horrible rush of regret. What had she done? This wasn't who she was anymore! She didn't blur lines with colleagues in hospital hallways and gamble with a career she'd rebuilt one careful, disciplined day at a time.

And yet, beneath the panic and her spiraling self-reproach, was a far more dangerous thought she really didn't want to admit to.

She hadn't meant to kiss him…but some long-buried part of her had very much wanted to.

CHAPTER SIX

JESS WAS SITTING alone at a small table near the cafeteria windows. She had a paper cup cradled in her hands as she gazed at something beyond the limits of the parking lot.

Nolan felt his heart pick up a beat at the sight of her. It had been two days since that secret kiss in the consultation room. With so many doctors taking vacation while their kids were out of school, Nolan had been working extra hours and hadn't crossed paths with Jess. So, their paths had not crossed at work since that night.

Jess had her hair pulled back in a tidy low bun instead of her usual ponytail. It emphasized the long angle of her neck, and her perfectly straight posture made her look like a ballerina at rest. But the cartoon characters on her scrub top had Jess's flare written all over.

Nolan ordered a grilled chicken Caesar wrap, then poured himself a fresh coffee and headed toward Jess's table.

"May I join you?"

She looked up, startled, then smiled. But it wasn't the megawatt smile Nolan was used to. "Sure. Please."

Nolan took his place at the table. When settled, they casually chatted about some crossover cases from the ED to pediatrics, and commiserated on how Radiology's issues with one of their X-ray machines was creating a backlog in their caseloads.

Jess was perfectly pleasant and friendly, but her usual spark was missing. She laughed or agreed at the right moments, but her feelings never quite reached her eyes.

"You seem a little off, Jess," Nolan said, unable to ignore her muted responses. "Everything okay?"

Jess sighed as she circled the rim of her cup with her finger. "I've just been thinking about some things."

Nolan felt the sick certainty that he'd crossed a line, professionally and personally, with Jess. Kissing her had been impulsive, maybe even selfish, and completely unfair to Jess. Just when they were starting to find common ground, he had gone and made everything more complicated.

"The kiss?" he prompted. She nodded. "Right. I just don't think I can date someone I work with," she said. "My job is everything to me. It's where I feel competent, where all my friends are, and I love it here. I don't want to destabilize that."

Her confirmation landed like a physical blow.

Nolan felt it in his chest first—a hollow, sinking

sensation—as Jess's careful tone made the situation clear. He had crossed a boundary with her. Everything he should have known came rushing back. Evan, the rumors, the way hospital gossip could chew through people long after the truth stopped mattering.

Shame followed close on its heels. Kissing her in the consult room hadn't been romantic. It had been reckless. It had pressed directly on every defense she'd built to survive this place, and now he'd given her another reason to keep him at arm's length.

In his impulsive move to connect with her, he had only driven her further away. So, he did what he did best.

He nodded—small, precise, professional—like she was walking him through new pediatric data instead of quietly drawing a line he knew not to cross. And fought to keep the sharp, personal sting of it from drowning out every word she said.

"These are my hard-won lessons from dating Evan." Her mouth curved into a rueful smile. "I knew it wasn't a good idea to date a colleague, even if he hadn't been married. But I got too optimistic that I could keep work and life separate. Turns out, the hospital has its own social ecosystem. Whatever happens to one of us is known by all of us."

Nolan couldn't disagree with her. He had heard more about every marriage, birth, bankruptcy, and promotion amongst his team than he had ever cared to know. In Jess's case, a breakup that went so bad was going to keep the gossip lines humming for months.

"I hope you understand."

Nolan felt the quiet sting of it land deep in his gut. She was being kind—too kind—giving him a way to retreat without having to admit how badly he'd misread the moment. He didn't know what had come over him, only that working with her had revealed something he hadn't expected: the rare satisfaction of watching two different ways of seeing the world interlock to make patients safer. The realization had reached him before language did—registering low and warm in his body, unmistakably right in a way he still didn't have words for. "I do," he said, but it was more reflex than truth.

She hesitated before adding, "I can still be your fake fiancée this weekend if you like. After all, we have coordinating attire now."

He smiled and laughed along like he meant it. Her offer was strangely generous—maybe intended to show that she wasn't pushing him away entirely.

But he knew what she was doing—trying to give him a way to protect his ego after an embarrassing misread of her feelings for him. Or, more precisely, her *lack* of romantic feelings for him.

Nolan pushed the sting away until his trusted mask slipped back in place. "I'd like that," he said, delivering his best, most reassuring doctor smile. "But only if you are sure."

"I'm sure," she said, standing and gathering her things. "See you upstairs, Nolan."

She left him in the wake of her gardenia perfume and with a bitter, cold coffee for company. His Caesar wrap finally arrived, distracting him from how empty the table felt when she was gone.

Her words landed soft, like the last warm rays of sunlight on a late summer afternoon. But all Nolan heard was the space between each syllable. She was pulling back. It was obvious from the careful distance of her tone and how she was easing herself away from him. The fragile peace they had started to build was shaky now, and maybe her desire to pose as his fake fiancée for the wedding, as well. Her pulling away wouldn't just complicate his family problem. It would follow them straight back into the hospital, into consults and case handoffs and split-second decisions that depended on trust instead of self-consciousness.

This was his fault.

The sharp rush of self-reproach cut through him. Kissing her had been reckless—an uncharacteristic mistake born of relief and connection. But mistakes could be corrected. Systems could be stabilized. Damage could be contained.

He just needed to shift back into familiar territory: professional and careful.

And make sure that what happened in that consult room never happened again.

The patient in room twelve was a little kid who should have been in school. Not under fluorescent lights with a pulse ox clipped to his toe.

Ten-year-old male, abdominal pain, low-grade fever, guarding. Rule out appendicitis.

Jess was waiting at the foot of the bed when Nolan walked in, one hip braced against the bed frame and a tablet in hand. She had exchanged her ballerina bun for a low-slung ponytail.

"Nolan," she greeted him, but she didn't look up from the screen.

He shook hands with the mother, knelt beside the bed so he wasn't looming, and introduced himself as casually as he could. He didn't have the same easy-breezy way with kids like Jess did, but they seemed to trust his methodical ways and total honesty.

Jess watched him as he worked, her attention just a tad too polite. Her smile hovered but never quite settled. She seemed too careful, faintly awkward, as if she wasn't sure where to put her hands or her eyes anymore. The whole thing felt painfully familiar: the kind of professional distance he'd spent six months deliberately building with her. How long had he told himself that if she could only rein in that perpetually apple-pie sunshine of hers, they'd work together just fine?

But now that he had what he wanted, he just missed her spark.

"How long since he ate?" Nolan asked.

"Nothing since last night," the mom said, voice tight. "He said he felt sick at breakfast, so—"

"Any vomiting?" Nolan asked, scanning the kid's face.

The boy shook his head and winced at the movement.

Jess gave him the essentials in bullet points, like she'd written them in her head beforehand.

"Pain started periumbilical, migrated to RLQ. Low-grade temp at home. No diarrhea. No sick contacts. He's tender. He's not peritonitic. CBC shows mild leukocytosis. Urine clean. I ordered an ultrasound."

The old Jess wouldn't have been able to resist throwing a zinger in at the end. Something like *because I know how much you love a good scan.* Or his particular favorite: *looks like textbook appendicitis to me, but let's wait for the test results to say I told you so.*

But no zingers capped off her case presentation today.

Nolan looked at the kid again. The kid looked back, eyes glassy with that combination of fear and misery Nolan knew too well. He pressed his hand gently into the lower right quadrant, watching for involuntary guarding. The kid sucked in a breath and nodded, as if giving Nolan permission to believe him.

Nolan straightened slowly. "Good call on the ultrasound. If the appendix isn't visualized and his exam remains concerning, we'll talk about more imaging. How's his pain control?"

"Tylenol. I held off on anything stronger until you saw him."

"Good," he said. And it was. He and Jess were working together like they should, focused on what their patient needed and not their personal issues.

Jess lifted her tablet between them as Nolan started to speak, angling the screen so he could see the results.

"White count's up to fourteen," she said, scrolling. "Neutrophils are climbing, too—and his CRP just posted."

Nolan leaned in to follow the trend.

Their shoulders brushed. It was nothing. Barely a touch.

But Jess, startled, jerked away from him. The tablet slipped from her fingers before clattering to the floor.

"Oh—sorry." Her words came too fast as she dropped into a crouch to retrieve it, nearly knocking into the supply cart beside her. When she straightened, color had bloomed across her cheeks.

She didn't look at him.

"Ultrasound still isn't definitive," she said quietly, eyes fixed on the screen now back in her hands. "But with the leukocytosis and the left shift, I think we should call surgery and keep him NPO."

She was protecting herself, he knew that. Maybe protecting him too. But as he stood there reviewing a patient whose course he could predict with near certainty, Nolan had the unsettling thought that protocols were easy.

This—working beside her as if that kiss had meant nothing, after making the mistake of believing it had meant the same thing to her as it had to him—was going to be far harder to manage.

Nolan turned to the mother and explained what they were doing, why an ultrasound first, what they were watching for. He saw the relief in her shoulders when he said, "We're going to take good care of him," and he felt the familiar little click inside himself—the sense of competence, purpose, control.

Control had always been enough for him. So, why wasn't it today?

When he finished, Jess nodded, already moving toward the door. "I'll message you with imaging."

Nolan followed her out into the corridor, because the consult wasn't complete without closing the loop, but also because he couldn't make himself leave Jess's orbit.

"I'll be in clinic until noon," he said. "If you need me."

Her smile was polite, but a little too quick. A token gesture meant to satisfy social code rather than connect with him. The hollow pit he felt in his gut surprised him.

Jess shifted the tablet against her hip, fumbled the edge, caught it again. "I'll message you when the ultrasound's read," she added, glancing past his shoulder toward the hallway instead of at him.

"Okay." She wasn't shutting him out. She was trying—awkwardly—to keep things smooth.

Jess turned to go. Her ponytail brushed the collar of her scrubs as she pivoted away.

Nolan stepped after her before he could stop himself.

"Jess."

She startled, just a little, and turned back. He braced for her familiar spark. The dry retort, or that quick look of hers that dared him to keep up.

"Yes?"

His heart sank. Her expression was open and pleasant, waiting to hear what he would say next. She wasn't guarded or cold. She just wasn't Jess either.

Any hopes he had that the carefulness he had seen in Jess during their cafeteria chat would stay in the cafeteria were fast being dashed. There was a distance between them now, and it wasn't going away on its own. It could complicate every consult and handoff they would have in the future. Make it harder to trust each other's judgment when it mattered.

"Never mind," he said, working hard to keep

his tone neutral. "Just let me know when the ultrasound's back."

She nodded once—even that was too formal for Jess—and turned away.

And then she was gone, and he felt so left behind.

Nolan took the elevator back to the seventh floor where his office, a sanctuary waited. Maybe there he could find some respite from his restless energy.

He sat at his desk and tried to read emails, but the words just wouldn't register in his brain. He watered his plants, dusted his bookshelf, tried to catch up on the filing that he always neglected.

But he could find no escape from feeling shut out. He hated that sensation. He'd felt it too many times in his youth. All those years of wanting to be seen and celebrated for who he was. Even more hours spent pushing himself to be the best—just for a chance at an attaboy as he shuttled between his brother's football practices and events.

Damn, he hadn't thought about those memories in years. Before this ridiculous fake fiancée fiasco, his life had run like a train on a schedule. He was in charge, respected, and relentlessly disciplined. Filled with a quiet certainty that he was doing everything right.

He missed that guy!

Now he felt unraveled and rudderless, not sure what direction to go.

The scientist in him said there had to be a way to solve this riddle. He paused in his pacing of his office to consider what he knew.

Her hesitance had landed somewhere deeper than logic. It stirred an old, familiar ache in his heart. That feeling that no matter how hard he tried, he had missed the mark. And that meant he was unworthy of her trust.

There had to be some way to prove to her that what happened in the consult room was an aberration. A single, reckless misstep. Not a pattern or a threat to her career.

And then find the way back to the easy professional rhythm they'd started to build: the shared glances over labs, the quiet handoffs, the growing confidence that they were stronger working together than clashing over their differences. Get back to being colleagues who trusted each other. Who maybe even were becoming friends.

Nolan was a master at earning what did not come easily to him. He had earned his father's respect by excelling at something other than sports. He could earn this too. He just had to show Jess—quietly, consistently, and without asking anything from her in return—that she could trust him again.

Feeling considerably cheered, Nolan found a clean legal pad, uncapped his fountain pen, and got to work. He wrote, "Jess Hayes—Known Data Points" across the top of the pad, and then began his list.

* * *

Jess was halfway through triaging her inbox when her phone buzzed again. She frowned down at the screen. It was a calendar invite from Nolan.

Observation Session: Pediatric Therapy Dog Pilot—Behavioral Sciences Unit

She stared at it, thumb hovering uselessly over the accept button. It was hard to ignore the unusual nature of the meeting. Not a grand rounds reminder or a device demo. Something different and totally unexpected from Nolan.

She'd heard about the pilot—from the nurses, mostly. It was an initiative from the Child Life team, who were dedicated to improving the pediatric hospital experience.

Emergency medicine didn't touch programs like this. Her job was to stabilize and ship patients off to the appropriate department.

And Nolan didn't usually show up for soft-edged projects at all.

Before she could overthink it, she tapped Accept.

Now she stood at the back of a small sunlit consultation room in Behavioral Sciences, hands folded loosely in front of her. Nolan leaned against the wall beside her, his arms crossed.

A soft golden retriever padded into the room, nails clicking faintly on the vinyl floor.

Jess felt her chest loosen before she could stop it. The dog's coat was warm, like the color of honey.

His tail moved like a slow, lazy fan, as if he understood exactly how fragile this room was.

On the couch across from them, a little girl, no more than five, was curled tightly into her mother's lap. Her face was buried in her mother's sweater, one small sneaker dangling and tapping nervously against the cushion.

The child-life coordinator lowered herself to a stool.

"This is Lucy," she explained to the medical staff who had come to observe. "She's been with our oncology team on and off for the past year. Acute lymphoblastic leukemia."

Jess's stomach tightened.

"She's had multiple admissions for treatment," the coordinator continued, "and several hospitalizations for infections during chemotherapy. Understandably, she associates medical settings with pain and separation from her family."

Lucy didn't look up.

"We're hoping that a therapy dog program can help children like Lucy tolerate care with less distress."

Jess shifted her weight. A familiar, helpless ache pressed into her chest. Hospital stays weren't easy on anyone, especially young patients who couldn't understand the painful testing and why they had to be separated from their home, school, and everything that felt familiar and safe.

The handler knelt a few feet away from the couch. "Lucy, this is Moby."

Moby lowered himself to the floor at once. He rested his chin on his paws and waited.

Lucy pressed her face harder into her mother's stomach.

Jess let out a breath without realizing it. "Oh, poor thing," she whispered.

She leaned closer to Nolan without thinking. "I remember her," she said softly. "She came through the ED a couple of times. Neutropenic fevers. Line infection, once."

I never get to see what happens after I stabilize them.

She lifted her eyes. Nolan was already looking at her. Not with his professional half smile or polite attentiveness.

Something quieter. And, if she could believe it, more open.

The small, unsettling warmth bloomed in her chest. Why had he invited her? He had to know this program would never intersect with the ED. She wouldn't sit on its committees. Wouldn't help design its metrics. Wouldn't be part of its rollout.

So this wasn't operational. Which meant…what?

It's personal.

The realization slid in sideways. A bit unwelcome, because things were already so complicated for them.

Maybe this was his way of smoothing over the mess they'd made in the consult room.

That kiss…the memory of it made her stomach drop. She still didn't know who had closed that final inch.

If she was being honest, she suspected it had been her.

The pull she felt to him had felt so real in that moment. So obvious and meaningful.

But it wasn't. She was just building stories out of glances and shared adrenaline.

No more, she had decided. No more reading into what wasn't actually there. From now on, she would keep her feet on the ground and her head out of the clouds.

And yet, here she was, at Nolan's invitation. Standing in a therapy session she had no professional reason to attend.

What does it mean?

Maybe nothing. Or maybe more. Maybe he had chosen this because he knew she cared about trauma-aware care. Or because he had seen how much moments of quiet connection with patients mattered to her.

Was this his attempt to connect to her?

Jess mentally threw up her hands. *Get a grip, Hayes!*

Nolan didn't feel what she felt. If he did, he would have said something by now. He wasn't the type to linger in an emotional gray zone.

Nolan was about timelines, deliverables, clean outcomes.

If he wanted her, he would tell her. Possibly with bullet points.

He would not invite her to a therapy dog session and hope she decoded his hidden message.

Jess's musings were interrupted by the appearance of Lucy's tiny hand slipping out from her cocoon. She froze.

Lucy's face stayed buried in her mother's stomach—but her fingers reached, trembling, until they brushed the silky fringe of Moby's ear. The dog didn't move. He was so good, so still, so patient. He simply stayed where he was, letting Lucy's fingers curl into his fur and explore what she found.

Jess's breath caught. She pressed two fingers to her lips. *Don't cry*, she willed herself.

But it was pretty hard not to when Lucy slowly unwound herself from her mother's lap so she could crouch in front of Moby. And wrap both arms around Moby's neck.

When Moby leaned into her without shifting his weight, Jess felt something break open in her chest. Before she could stop herself, she glanced at Nolan. She was braced for the familiar impassive calm. The same one she ran into every time she argued for accommodations, for flexibility, for anything that lived outside a flowchart.

But it wasn't there. Instead, to her surprise, Nolan was smiling. Nothing huge. Just a soft, gentle smile that said he saw it too. A patient, steady dog had just succeeded—without medication or protocol—where everything else had failed.

Something warm and unsteady flickered in her heart. Before she could think what it meant, her phone beeped and shattered the spell.

Quality Improvement—Pediatric Throughput Review

Jess grimaced.

"I'm so sorry," she whispered. "I have a meeting to attend."

Nolan leaned back on his heels, hands buried in his coat pockets. The smile faded as he said, "No problem. I'll walk you out."

They waited in silence at the elevator.

"I really appreciate you inviting me," Jess said. "It was…honestly incredible to see this in action. I think it's going to do a lot of good."

Nolan nodded. "I do too."

She tried to be satisfied with that, but something tugged at her.

"Just out of curiosity…" she said lightly. "Why did you invite me? It's not exactly your normal…"

"Modus operandi?" he finished.

She smiled. "Right."

He shrugged. "I don't know. I just thought you might be interested."

She bit her lip as a quiet disappointment settled

in her stomach. He wasn't telling her everything, but she didn't know why.

The elevator doors slid open.

Jess stepped inside. Then stopped. She simply couldn't ignore the curiosity that was buzzing about her brain.

Her hand shot out and pressed the door-open button, making the elevator chime.

"Nolan."

He looked up, eyebrow lifting in mild surprise.

Her heart thudded once, hard.

"Do you ever talk about yourself?" She tried to keep her tone light, even as something tight coiled in her chest.

"There's not much to tell."

She studied him, wishing he wasn't such a closed book.

"It just feels like I'm always guessing where you are," she said gently. "And I don't like guessing."

"Ask anything you want," he said.

"Okay." She plucked at a loose thread on her skirt. "Why did you need a fake fiancée for your wedding?"

Nolan didn't move an inch, and for a minute, she thought he was planning his reply. But in the end, he disappointed her.

"It's complicated. That's all."

Acceptance settled over her with a quiet finality. Nolan wasn't going to open that door, not now, maybe not ever. Any thoughts that she had that he was trying to connect with her in some way were just her typical pie-in-the-sky thinking.

Nolan was pulling back, just like she was. He knew they had gone too far with that kiss, and that professional boundaries had been crossed.

This was a good thing. Nolan was letting her know where his boundaries were. They could connect over patient care—even share a heartwarming experience like this therapy dog session. But when it came to knowing Nolan—*really* knowing him—that was never going to happen. He wanted to keep the most important parts of himself locked away, neat and protected, the way he organized everything else in his life.

CHAPTER SEVEN

Your ring repair is done. I can drop it off if you like.

IN HINDSIGHT, MAYBE THE therapy dog session had been a mistake.

It had seemed like a good place to start getting back on track with Jess. The list he made about Jess included everything he knew about her so far. She loved animals. She was always thinking about her patients beyond their immediate medical needs. She was kind, well-liked, and vivacious.

He didn't quite know how to cobble all that together into a road back to trust. Until he received the invite to observe a therapy dog session. This, he thought, was something Jess might love. Just the right blend of professional distance with a modest dash of personal connection.

And that part *had* worked—maybe too well? For a brief moment, it had felt easy again. Like the beginning of something steadier than the awkward truce they'd been circling since the kiss.

But as soon as she had reached for something more personal, he had clammed up like he always did. Instead of smoothing things over, he had managed to amplify the distance between them. All so he could protect his image of being the smartest guy in the room.

He should have known how that would go over with Jess. He *did* know. He'd met her father, had seen how a man could be present and yet not there. He knew exactly what Evan had taken from her by parceling out affection like it was optional.

Jess had been surrounded by men who expected her to be strong because it was convenient for them, who gave her less than she needed and called it enough. Nolan had thought he was protecting his dignity by staying contained, but for Jess, it was just another closed door.

Nolan climbed the steps to Jess's apartment—the repaired engagement ring tucked in his jacket pocket. She opened the door with a warm, familiar smile and stepped aside without hesitation. "Right on time," she said lightly. "I was wondering when that would be ready." He handed her the small box, watching as she opened it and slid the ring onto her finger. It fit perfectly and she turned her hand to admire it with an approving nod. "This will work great for the weekend.

"Do you want something to drink?" she asked, already moving toward the kitchen. "Coffee or wine?"

"Wine's fine," he replied, taking a seat.

She poured as they chatted about the wedding logistics. "Where are we staying?"

"The guest room at my family home. It has twin beds, so…" He trailed off so he didn't have to state the obvious: that she probably wanted as much physical distance from him as possible.

She nodded, grateful but composed, and Nolan understood exactly what she was bracing for: not temptation, not awkwardness—but survival. She wanted to get through this strange adventure weekend with her dignity intact so she could put everything that had happened between them behind her.

Whatever spark had flared that night at the hospital, he had done a damn fine job of dousing it when he failed to meet her halfway.

"I brought you something," he said, reaching into his bag.

Her eyes brightened immediately. "Something *else*?" she teased, glancing down at the ring on her finger. "Because honestly, the engagement ring was enough for me."

"The ring is for the wedding. This," Nolan said, pulling a vinyl album from his backpack, "is for you."

For a second she simply stared at the album cover, as if her brain needed time to catch up. "No way," she breathed. "Harbor & Pine?" She looked up at him, stunned. "I told you I lost this when I moved to San Francisco. Do you have any idea how rare this is?"

Oh yeah, he knew. He had spent countless hours combing collector sites, auctions, and for sale listings, chasing dead ends until one finally worked out.

"Oh my gosh—we have to listen." She crossed the room in a rush, dragging her record player closer to the coffee table, handling the vinyl with reverence as she set the needle in place. The opening notes filled the room, warm and familiar, and she turned back to him, eyes soft in a way he hadn't seen in days. "This was really thoughtful," she said quietly. "Thank you."

Nolan watched her, framed by the soft glow of the table lamp, eyes closed as the music wrapped around her. The corners of her mouth lifted in the faintest smile, completely absorbed. She looked unguarded, relaxed in a way he rarely saw during her urgent work at the hospital.

It struck him how different she was from the woman he thought he'd known. He had thought Jess was a mess of energy and chaos, but the more their engagement ruse forced them together, the harder it became to ignore their symmetry. How carefully Jess curated her cheerfulness, how deliberately he hid behind competence—and how much they were both, in their own ways, wearing armor instead of letting themselves be seen.

Beneath that realization was a desire to protect this side of her. To be part of her calm as well as her storm. For the first time, he understood why this wasn't just about attraction—it was about wanting to know her entirely, even the parts she'd never let anyone else see.

She opened her eyes as the last notes faded, letting the silence settle between them. Nolan leaned back slightly, his gaze tracing the contours of her face.

"You asked me why I needed a fiancée for Connor's wedding," he said quietly. He took a breath and willed himself to finish. On the drive to her apartment, he had practiced his monologue repeatedly. Ready to reveal the childhood failures that had charted the trajectory of his life, and the feelings of inadequacy and failure that kept him feeling like an outsider to his family.

But now, sitting here in her living room, her gaze expectant and kind, he fought to break down the image he had cultivated for so long. Jess only knew him as Dr. Nolan Stone. Uptight and rigid, yes, but also competent and in control. A person of authority who could be trusted because he left nothing to chance.

Telling her the truth about why he needed a fiancée would blow up that image and leave her with…what? The real him? What was she going to do with that?

And how on earth would that help them protect their professional connection? It wouldn't—not at all.

He swirled the wine in his glass, the ruby hues breaking apart and reforming in a slow, mesmerizing kaleidoscope. Everything he was doing was about work—protecting their images and connection so they could work together day after day.

He took a long look at Jess. At the whimsical sweep of her dress, the bright, hopeful light in her eyes. For so long, he had dismissed her optimism and flair as annoying distractions from work. But the truth was they were badges of her courage. Where he had made up a mirage to escape judgment, she had leaned into who she was and let everyone else catch up.

He cleared his throat. "Um, it's just something that started as a little joke. And then it got out of hand, you know?"

Jess's expression was expectant, waiting for the next reveal so his story made sense. So *he* made sense.

When she realized he had no more explanation to give, she quickly licked her lips, then took another sip of wine. "Okay…"

He knew it didn't explain everything, but he tried to save face as best he could.

"So, now you know, Jess. I'm not perfect." He let his mouth curve into a wry smile. "I alphabetize my spice rack and get irrationally annoyed when it's out of order. Plus, I've burned pasta more than once because I was answering work emails."

Jess felt something loosen in her chest as Nolan finished speaking, as if a door she hadn't known how to find had finally been opened from the inside. He wasn't telling her everything—she knew that. But still, his willingness to try to connect with her made him look different to her now—less polished, more exposed—his usual composure edged with a vulnerability that was downright sexy.

Jess smiled slowly, feeling some of the tension ease for the first time that evening. "That's nothing, Nolan," she said, tilting her head, a spark lighting her eyes. "This week alone I forgot my badge twice, reheated the same cup of coffee three times and never drank it, and—oh yeah—got stuck in the vending machine again."

His laugh came easily, warm and familiar, and she took it as encouragement. "Oh—and I wore two different socks to work on Tuesday," she added. "On purpose. I was daring someone to notice." For a moment, it felt like old times—their lighthearted sparring testing the boundaries of the attraction between them. Only now, there were no sharp edges or frustration. Just the warmth of recognition and the discovery that they had been on the same side of the argument all along.

"Anyway," Nolan said, stuffing his hands in the pockets of his college hoodie. His voice shifted to a more serious tone. "I need you to know that if you still want to go to the wedding this weekend, you can trust me. And that I trust you—with who I really am, not just the polished version. Though fair warning, you might see that guy hanging around the wedding from time to time." A faint, hopeful smile touched his mouth. "With any luck," he added lightly, "maybe we'll even have a little fun."

"Thank you, Nolan," Jess said, rising to her feet. He followed suit and she reached to give him a hug. She meant it to be an expression of acceptance and friendship, but the instant she felt his arms wrap around her, something shifted in her. The attraction she had been trying to deny ever since that stolen kiss at the hospital roared back into a huge bonfire. All she wanted to do was tilt her chin up and feel Nolan's mouth on hers again, making the world melt away into a hazy abstract of feelings and desires.

Jess swallowed hard and stepped out of his embrace. She would not mess this up by letting her ridiculous dreams and desires take over. Nolan had come here to make things right—as her colleague and her friend. She didn't need to muck that up with her endless thoughts of possibilities.

Jess walked him to the door, her fingers brushing his as she held it open. The heat between them was sudden and unmistakable, and she saw the way he stiffened slightly, as if he hadn't expected this—like neither of them had. Her pulse kicked up, and she leaned just a fraction closer, letting the tension fill the narrow space between them.

Nolan stepped into the hallway, drawing a bracing breath before he turned back to her. "Good night, Jess," he said with a rueful smile.

"Night, Nolan."

She willed him to walk away so she could go back in her apartment, close the door, and do something—anything—to keep her mind and body busy and out of trouble.

Because she was finding it almost impossible to ignore the sensations that were throbbing through her body and mind. Something about Nolan pulled at her on every level, and despite her vow to stick to her professional lane, she felt a terrible sense of urgency to cross the distance between them, grab the lapels of his jacket, and pull him to her.

For some reason, he wasn't leaving like he should. Something was flickering in his eyes as his gaze raked her face. The moment stretched between them, fragile and electric.

Without knowing she was going to do it, she reached across the shallow distance between them. Her hand found his chest, and she felt his heat radiating beneath her palm. Feeling hypnotized, she raised herself on tiptoes, and leaned into him. Her eyes fluttered shut as she surrendered to whatever was going to happen next.

Nolan's hand found her waist just as a phone buzzed between their bodies. Jess felt it before she heard it. Something soft and warm rose in her chest, then faltered like a breath cut short.

Nolan stilled before he pulled his phone from his

back pocket. With the screen lit in the dark hallway, she could see the caller's name. Mom.

It was almost poetic, this reminder of how she came to be standing outside of her apartment with Nolan. Not because of attraction that either had acted on independently, but because of a ruse that had been created from a misunderstanding.

The almost kiss collapsed inside her—heat cooling, hope folding in on itself with quiet, practiced efficiency. Why did she keep doing this? Imagining connections where there were none? Grasping at straws as if she were in distress and Nolan was her rescuer?

Nolan's jaw tightened. His thumb hovered.

"I—" he started, then stopped.

Jess took a small step back without meaning to. "You should take it," she said softly. The call was her salvation, saving her from another embarrassing mistake.

He looked at her, something apologetic flickering across his face. Then the phone buzzed a second time.

And the space where his mouth had been a breath away from hers widened until the moment was gone.

Jess stepped out of the car and paused to take in Nolan's family home. The house was a two-story Craftsman with wide wraparound porches, weathered wood beams, and tall windows that reflected the waning summer sunlight. It was quite beautiful, full of old California charm and quiet affluence.

"Oof—!"

Jess turned to see Nolan double over just before a football bounced off the gravel and skittered under the car. A pack of sweaty kids soon swarmed them, yelling "Uncle Nolan! Uncle Nolan!" in unison.

Jess's eyebrows shot up. "Ambushed upon arrival. I didn't see that one coming."

Nolan straightened, breathless. "It's family tradition." Then he was being tugged away by two of the kids, just before Jess felt a little hand take hers and tug her toward the wide grassy lawn, where a menagerie of adults, kids and teenagers were playing a spirited game of football.

"Wait!" she laughed, but the boy with red hair and round glasses just tugged harder. "I'm not dressed for…oh, never mind!" She kicked off her sandals, very glad she hadn't worn a dress for their trip to the Stone family vineyard.

Joining the game, she and Nolan darted across the sprawling lawn, dodging, weaving, and lunging for the bright orange flag pinned to each other's belts. Laughter erupted every time someone slipped on the grass or collided with a teammate, and Jess felt the electric sting of Nolan brushing past her as they sprinted side by side. She grabbed for his flag, missed, then pivoted, laughing, as he spun away with a triumphant grin.

The ball flew from one hand to the next, players shouting and calling plays. The sun seemed suspended in the sky, unwilling to set until the final play had been called. She felt its warmth on her back as the deep green lawn seemed to stretch out around them forever.

Maybe she admired the idyllic vineyard setting too long, because suddenly she was flying sideways, suspended in the air. Strong arms wrapped around her waist and twisted her to the side, so that when she finally landed, it was Nolan's body who took the impact while he cradled her for the crash.

"Sorry," he said against her neck, making her hair stir with his breath. "Connor can't resist tackling me for real every chance he gets."

His chest felt warm and solid against her back, making it hard to break away from his embrace. She rolled to her feet, then offered him a hand to get up too. "You warned me that your family takes their sports seriously. Now I see what you mean!"

"Right?" Nolan said, his face almost boyish with mischievous charm.

Nolan's family were loud, competitive, and trash-talking like this was the final playoff game of the season. She loved every zesty, sweaty minute and kept up surprisingly well considering she didn't even know if football was played in quarters, halves, or periods. She managed to dart past

Nolan's nephews, grab a flag off his brother mid-spring, and spent her free time high-fiving the smallest cousin like they'd known each other for years.

And then someone was shouting from the porch, "Get inside this minute, you wild banshees! Rehearsal dinner starts in an hour! I'm not doing everything by myself!"

Everyone scattered this way and that, grabbing her luggage, fetching her shoes. Jess, flushed and now covered in grass, kept up as best she could, following the flow of bantering, jostling bodies into the house where she met his mother, Abigail. She was set at the kitchen counter with a proper glass of wine and within arm's reach of a tantalizing array of appetizers, dips, and snacks.

Jess offered to help with dinner, so Abigail gave her the job of cutting vegetables while they chatted. Nolan had kept her under lock and key far too long and she wanted Jess all to herself for a while.

"So, what is your secret, Jess? You've got Nolan smiling like a fool," Abigail said, refilling her wineglass. "I don't think I've seen him laugh this much in years."

Jess smiled, a little self-conscious. "He…uh, he's easy to make laugh."

Mrs. Stone's eyes twinkled. "Is that right? I always thought he saved his smiles for victories. Always trying so hard to be perfect, you know?" She paused, studying Jess with curiosity and warmth.

"So…what do you do to him? How did you get past all that armor?"

Jess laughed softly. "I think I just let him forget he has to be perfect for a little while."

"Oh, I like that," Mrs. Stone said, nodding. "You know, Nolan was always the quiet one growing up. Always the kid who studied while his brother was out scoring touchdowns. I worried he'd never find someone who could see him for himself…not just the achievements."

Jess felt a little flutter. "He's pretty careful with his reputation, that's for sure."

Mrs. Stone reached out and patted her hand. "Yes, he is. But I can tell—he's happier around you. You bring out the part of him he keeps tucked away. That's a gift, Jess. Treat it well."

Jess blinked, touched. "I will."

The back door opened and soon the quiet space Jess had shared with Abigail was filled with rambunctious laughter and chatter as Nolan and the others returned from setting up the backyard for the rehearsal dinner. Nolan's brother, Connor, was bigger and louder than Nolan, and apparently allergic to shirts with sleeves. Jess nibbled on flatbread while Connor recounted his "game-winning play" that, as far as Jess could tell, hadn't won anything. But he was amusing and his fiancée, Lauren, was sweet as honey.

Connor slung an arm around Nolan's shoulders. "So. Jess." He leaned in with a grin. "Tell us. Where'd my little brother propose? Cause I got money down that he can't top my private olive grove dinner proposal in Tuscany last summer." He looked over his shoulder, where his wife-to-be was leaning against the refrigerator. "What did I bet again?"

She rolled her eyes. "You bet two hundred imaginary dollars that Nolan's proposal involved a PowerPoint presentation."

Connor turned back to them, a wide grin making his cheeks turn red. "That's right! So, tell us the truth, Jess. How did my bro manage to sweep you off your feet?"

"Oh, leave her alone," Abigail said, turning the oven alarm off when it beeped. "She just got here, for Pete's sake. Give her a minute to catch her breath before you unleash the full Stone family experience on her."

Jess just laughed. 'It's fine,' she said. She thought that was the end of it, until she noticed Connor's face. He really did want to know how Nolan had proposed. And if his football bragging was any measure of his competitive streak, Nolan's coffee proposal story was in for a long night of ridicule.

Jess scanned the kitchen until she found Nolan's calm, brown eyes. She mimed driving a car while arching her eyebrow. *Grand theft auto story?*

Nolan must have read the question in her expression, because he shook his head no.

Please? she mouthed when Connor wasn't looking.

He gave her a look like *this is gonna be trouble*. But when Connor planted a loud, wet kiss on his cheek just for effect, Nolan apparently decided to go rogue.

"Actually, honey, why don't you tell him how we met instead?" The corner of his mouth curved in quiet amusement.

A silent understanding passed between them—playful and intimate. A little secret that only they shared.

"Okay, snookums. If you insist." And then she launched into the grand theft auto story.

The rowdy Stone family settled into a rapt audience, as she recounted how Nolan had been hauled off to jail. How she couldn't stop thinking about him and his beautiful eyes. How she raided her retirement account to pay his bond, then they walked the streets of San Francisco as the sun came up.

"Then we walked arm in arm, watching San Francisco come to life with the scent of sourdough scenting the air…"

The entire kitchen was frozen and silent.

"Wait…what happened?" Lauren whispered.

Connor's eyes bulged. "The whole city smelled of sourdough?"

Nolan's mother dropped a serving spoon into a bowl of marinated olives while his father looked like he'd bitten into a lemon.

"And to think, one little car accident led to all this."

Nolan was next to her now, and she hooked her arm into his, gazing up at him with all the adoration she could muster.

Every head swiveled toward Nolan. No one said a word.

"You didn't have your license?" Abigail asked, incredulous.

He coughed. "I…uh…panicked. Left my wallet in my gym bag."

And then, all at once, the spell broke and everyone was talking and laughing and telling Nolan they had no idea he was such a romantic and what a wonderful person Jess was, bailing him out of jail like that.

"Yeah," Nolan coughed to hide his laugh. "She's amazing."

As they headed toward the garden for the rehearsal dinner, Nolan took her hand. "We probably shouldn't have done that. But it was fun."

Jess slipped her fingers through his. "I couldn't let him have the coffee proposal story." She did her best to mimic Connor's hearty, overly masculine tone. "So little bro, did you *grind* your way into her heart? *Espresso* your feelings? You never would have heard the end of it."

The rehearsal dinner was set in a rustic hall at the edge of the vineyard, strings of fairy lights zigzagging across the exposed beams and casting a soft glow over polished wooden tables. The scent of rosemary and roasted garlic mingled with the faint tang of wine from nearby barrels, and Jess felt a flutter in her chest as she stepped through the doorway. She had to remind herself—fake fiancée, fake smiles, fake engagement. But for now, she let herself breathe it in.

"Jess, come sit here," Nolan's mother called, waving her over to the head table. His father, tall and imposing but warm in manner, rose to shake her hand, giving her a smile that somehow made her nerves ease. "It's so good to finally meet you."

"You too," Jess said, trying to sound natural, though her pulse was still racing. She felt Nolan's hand brush against hers under the table—small, grounding, reassuring.

"Connor and I are so happy you and Nolan could make it to the wedding," Lauren said warmly, her boys tugging at her hand as they clambered onto chairs beside her. "These are my little troublemakers," she said, giving Jess a conspiratorial grin.

Jess laughed softly. "It's great to meet all of you. I can already tell this is a lively family."

"You two make a gorgeous couple," Lauren said. "Everyone has been dying to meet the girl who stole Nolan's heart."

Jess raised an eyebrow, trying not to laugh. "I don't know about stealing it. There's not too much that gets past Nolan."

She caught Nolan's eye, and the hint of a smirk

on his lips made her heart stutter. Even pretending, there was something easy about this.

Over dinner, the conversation flowed in warm, teasing waves. His mother asked questions about her work and her family, listening intently, genuinely interested, nodding at every word Jess offered. His father shared stories of Nolan's stubbornness as a kid—how he refused to leave the library until he'd solved a math problem—and Jess couldn't help but laugh at the image. Connor chimed in, rolling his eyes at the memory, and Lauren's boys interrupted with excited chatter about the vineyard's animals, which had everyone smiling and shaking their heads.

Jess bit into the rosemary focaccia that Nolan nudged her way, then groaned with delight. "My gosh, this is amazing," she swooned. "Your mom is an incredible cook."

"She's spoiled us all," Nolan said softly, eyes flicking to Jess with that quiet intensity she recognized. She felt a slow bloom of warmth low in her chest. Even under the guise of fake engagement, it was easy to forget the roles they were playing when he looked at her like that.

Jess felt a nudge at her side. She glanced at Nolan, who had just poured her a bit more wine, and their eyes met.

He raised an eyebrow slightly, that familiar half smile playing at his lips, and she felt the familiar rush of heat in her chest. Just for a second, the barn seemed to shrink around them. No one else noticed, but they both knew the glance carried a secret: the playful tension, the unspoken acknowledgment that while their engagement was fake, the pull between them was very real.

Jess tipped her glass toward him. He returned the gesture, eyes softening, almost tender. For that moment, she allowed herself to imagine what it might feel like to actually be with him in real life. Sharing small, ordinary moments with Nolan every day and being part of milestone events like this as they grew older.

The moment broke when Nolan's mother clapped her hands. "Nolan! Don't make Jess blush at the table!" she teased, and laughter rippled around them. Jess caught Nolan's gaze one last time before turning back to the conversation, her heart still skipping, knowing they shared a secret spark that no one else could see.

Jess followed Nolan up the stairs to a room at the end of the hallway. Nolan turned the door handle and the thick oak door opened. Jess flipped on the overhead light.

It was…cozy. As soon as she stepped in, her heart sank a little. "Uh… Nolan?" she said, looking around.

He turned, his brow furrowing. "Yeah?"

She pointed toward the center of the room. "There's…just one bed."

Nolan's mouth twitched. He stepped fully into the room, setting his bag on the floor. "I guess my mom has done some redecorating. There used to be twin beds in here."

Jess laughed nervously, crossing her arms. "Well, that's okay." She looked around the space, trying to figure out a way for this to work. Sharing a bed felt way too dangerous after everything that had happened between them over the past few days. The spark of attraction she felt for Nolan was undeniable, but that didn't mean she was ready to change their relationship forever.

"I'll take the floor," Nolan said firmly. "I just need a few extra blankets. It'll be fine."

There weren't a lot of options here. Nolan was right—he could take the floor, or the armchair. But that was ridiculous. Why should he be uncomfortable all night when they were two grown adults?

"No way," she said quickly. "It's a queen, right? There's plenty of room." She kept her voice calm and neutral, but she couldn't ignore the coil of tension between them.

"I don't want you to be uncomfortable, Jess."

"I'm not," she lied. Jess swallowed, realizing that even saying it aloud didn't calm her racing heart. She placed her bag on the chair and moved toward the bed, trying to keep her stride confident. Nolan followed, carrying his own bag, and stopped at the edge of the mattress.

"Looks like we're going to have to…navigate

this," he said lightly, though there was a tension in his jaw, a controlled edge she hadn't seen before.

Jess perched on the far corner of the bed. "It's no big deal," she told him, wishing that felt true to her. "You take your side. I take mine. We sleep." She shrugged. "Easy."

He lowered his bag to the floor, and then paused. "You sure?"

"I'm sure," she pronounced with a definitive nod.

"Right," he said, settling down a foot or two away. But even as they tried to give each other space, the room felt smaller with each breath. Jess could feel the warmth radiating off him, smell the faint pine of his cologne mixing with the vineyard air drifting through the cracked-open window.

Minutes passed in a careful, tense silence as they checked their phones and fiddled with their luggage. Anything to avoid...*this*. And yet, every small movement sent sparks of tension coursing through her.

Jess sighed quietly to herself. *Great. One bed, fake engagement, and me with no idea how I'm going to not lose it.*

She changed in the bathroom, brushing her teeth extra hard as if they had done something wrong. She replayed everything she had learned about Nolan since coming to his family's vineyard. Especially what she had learned from Abigail.

In that moment, Jess realized that the Nolan she worked beside every day—the careful, controlled, relentlessly competent physician—was only half the story. The other half was still running from an old, familiar shame: the wound of having once disappointed his father, and the fear of ever being found lacking again.

Suddenly, the parts of him she had struggled to understand—the rigid devotion to protocol, the way he guarded his emotions, his instinct to retreat when things turned personal—no longer felt like professional distance. They felt like his armor, and she wanted to be the one to help him set it down.

And now, here she was—about to share a bed with him, close enough to feel the quiet heat of his presence, knowing there would be no hiding from what her body wanted. Understanding his vulnerabilities—the old shame he carried, the careful way he protected himself—only sharpened the pull. She braced her hands on the sink and willed herself to get some control over her racing pulse, and the terrifying thoughts of how little it would take for her to stop pretending she felt nothing at all.

Jess stepped out of the bathroom, then moved aside to make room for Nolan to have his turn. Quietly, she eased onto her side of the bed, careful to leave plenty of space between them, and adjusted the blanket around her.

He emerged a few minutes later, wearing a soft

gray Henley tee and plaid pajama bottoms. So different from his uniform attire at the hospital, and so very…appealing. She squeezed her eyes shut, willing herself to remember that in less than two days, they would return to San Francisco, her brief stint as Nolan's "fiancée" behind her. Her feelings, as churned up as they might be, were still just *her* feelings. Other than flirting a little over the rehearsal dinner, Nolan's feelings were as buttoned up as ever. She had to remember that, lest she make another mistake like she did in the hospital consult room.

But she couldn't resist casting one glance over her shoulder, and then wishing she hadn't. Nolan was tucked snug under the covers, an open book in his hands. He'd moved far over to his side to give her room, closer to the lamp so its faint glow cast soft shadows across his features.

He looked so unguarded and boyish. It was tempting to believe that here and now, in this space, Nolan might let down his guard with her.

"Good night," she whispered, and he looked up, offering a small smile.

"Good night, Jess," he murmured. Nothing more.

She turned off her lamp, plunging the room into darkness, and shut her eyes tight, trying to still the heat of longing that coursed through her body and the memory of their last, perfect kiss.

CHAPTER EIGHT

NOLAN WOKE ON his back, eyes half open, watching the slow, rhythmic sweep of the ceiling fan overhead, its soft whir anchoring him somewhere between sleep and awareness. For a few groggy seconds he didn't know where he was. The mattress didn't feel familiar, and the combination of old wood and lavender didn't smell like his town house at all.

Then it all came back, each memory settling in its place. His parents' house. His brother's wedding. The guest room, one bed, and…an unfamiliar warmth pressed along his side.

Nolan cast his glance sideways and found the source of the heat. Jess had rolled into him sometime in the night, her head tucked neatly into the crook of his arm. Her fingers were curled lightly against his chest.

His breath hitched. He held himself still, not wanting to shift and wake her and break this fragile connection. Instead, he lay there, heart thudding too loud, stunned by how intimate her sleeping weight felt against him.

It felt good to be her place of rest. Like she trusted him to keep her safe while she slept. Nolan let himself linger in the sensation. Nolan had earned many impressive accomplishments in his life. But earning Jess's trust—strong, capable Jess—was a prize he didn't know he wanted until this moment.

Sharing a bed with Jess had been…a lot. It had taken all his self-control to keep his eyeballs glued on his book. Not that he was reading—the book could have been upside down for all he cared. He had spent more time considering the curve of her hip than he had the plot of his book. *Touch her!* his brain had whispered-screamed. He imagined himself reaching out, laying a light hand on her hip. He imagined her rolling back to him with a sweet, seductive smile. He imagined everything that could come next.

But those were impossible thoughts. So, he'd stayed still, breathing through the wanting, honoring the fragile connection they had built over the past few weeks.

Suddenly, with no warning, someone was pounding at the door. Connor's voice followed, his booming baritone penetrating the thick oak door and the cozy cocoon they had created.

Jess jumped a little, which made her realize where she was: tucked in the alcove of Nolan's chest and arm. Instantly her cheeks flushed with embarrassment, and she jumped out of bed.

Nolan's gaze tracked her before he could stop himself, her oversized pink T-shirt slipping off one shoulder and a pair of soft, worn shorts riding up her thigh as she crossed the room. It wasn't the flash of skin that caught him so much as the easy, unguarded way she moved—sleep-rumpled and real. A quiet warmth settled low in his chest as he considered how this version of Jess—ordinary and close and completely within reach—felt far more dangerous than any kiss they'd ever shared.

"Rise and shine, sleepyheads! I'm getting hitched today!" Connor's laugh was hearty and jovial and oh so irritating.

"Mom made mimosas!" he called, his voice fading as he bounded down the stairs.

Jess and Nolan stared at each for a frozen minute, then broke out into laughter.

Nolan gently hushed her. "Shh, or he'll come back."

Jess's dark waves spilled across her shoulder and partially covered her face. Nolan felt an almost irresistible urge to swoop the errant hair away from her face and tuck it behind her ear.

Jess reached out and tugged a blanket from the bed and wrapped it around her shoulders. She settled at the foot of the bed, facing Nolan.

"You dreading today?" she asked, yawning and stretching.

Nolan tried to focus on her question, craving the distraction for a change. Before Jess had agreed to be his "fiancée," he had dreaded Connor's wedding for weeks. The comparisons, the expectations, the inevitable moments when he would not measure up to his brother's fame and achievement.

But now, knowing Jess would be there, a calm warmth spread through him. Her presence changed this event from a trial to be endured into a performance to enjoy. Because of her, he could relax, laugh at the improbable things that would happen, and maybe even have fun.

Her blanket slipped a bit, revealing the soft curve of her chest beneath the faded pink T-shirt. Nolan had to fight the instinct to look away—and the stronger one not to. He was suddenly, painfully aware of the quiet rise and fall of her breathing, of how easily his attention kept betraying him even when his better judgment was screaming for distance. But the ache in his chest was his alone. Jess had already made it clear she didn't feel this same dangerous pull back toward him.

Connor bellowed from below. Something about the last batch of blueberry pancakes.

Jess's eye widened. "I love blueberry pancakes," she whispered.

That was the exit ramp they both needed.

"You want to shower first, or eat?"

* * *

After breakfast, Jess took her time showering, letting the warm water and soapy bubbles wash away all the feelings and complications of a weekend that was just getting started.

Waking up next to Nolan had been a surprise, but she hadn't wanted to move right away. She had lain still, letting the steady weight of Nolan's arm around her seep into her bones, savoring his warmth.

She had wanted—more than she cared to admit—to close the last fraction of distance between them, to give in to the desire that had been building for weeks. But even as her pulse thrummed at the nearness, a thread of caution held her back. Nolan had made the effort to bridge the distance between them when he came to her apartment with the ring and finally shared who he was with her.

But breaking down walls wasn't the same as building a future. There were a lot of unknowns. After the wedding, there would be no reason to be in Nolan's orbit, let alone play make-believe fiancée. They would get back to normal—him on the pediatrics floor, her in the ED—with no need to see each other beyond working a case together.

These thoughts landed harder than she expected, leaving her with a soft grief she didn't quite know how to handle. This strange, borrowed closeness with Nolan had an expiration date, and she could already feel it ticking forward with every shared look. She told herself she should be relieved—that clean lines and safe distance were what she'd wanted all along. But the little ache in her chest whispered otherwise.

By the time she showered, dressed for the wedding, and rejoined Nolan, she had her smile back in place. She thought she had her feelings resolved, but when she rounded the corner, she sucked in an involuntary breath. He wore the pressed linen shirt she had selected for him open at the collar, with dark chinos instead of suit pants. His Napa Valley casual vibe was perfect for his brother's vineyard wedding.

Maybe she was an idiot. People had flings at weddings all the time. Why couldn't she enjoy a brief night of fantasy and escape with Nolan too? Just one teensy, tiny, one-night fling for the fun of it?

If only they weren't colleagues. If he were a trainer at her gym or someone from her apartment complex, she could give in and not second-guess herself about it so much.

Her father had poured the foundation, but Evan had taught her the hard lessons of how easily trust could be broken, and how long it took to put everything back together.

She wasn't willing to risk the connection she had with Nolan for a fleeting moment of passion. Crossing that line might satisfy desire, but it could also leave her exposed in ways she wasn't ready to face.

"Showtime," she whispered to herself, then came up and slipped her arm into his. He looked down in surprise, then relaxed into an easy grin that said he was happy to see her. She smiled back but soon had to break his gaze. Those ruinous brown eyes were going to do her in.

Just don't look at him, she vowed, as they began mixing and mingling with family. The afternoon became a blur of introductions and stories and congratulations, but underneath it all was a constant buzz of sexual frustration. It took all her concentration to stay focused on conversations.

A photographer called her and Nolan over for a family picture. Jess and Nolan wedged themselves in the middle row, between his aunt and a second or third cousin—Jess wasn't sure.

Jess smoothed her dress, stepping close to Nolan as the photographer called for a "natural, candid" shot. She could feel the heat radiating from him, subtle but impossible to ignore.

Nolan's aunt broke her pose to lean into Jess and Nolan's space. "Welcome to the family, Jess," she said with a huge smile. "I've been dying to hear how you two met."

"So…uh…" Nolan started, his hand awkwardly brushing hers as he adjusted the lapel of his suit. "We…met at—" He froze, eyes flicking up to hers, and she stifled a laugh. Had he really forgotten their grand theft auto story already?

"Well, it's a funny story," she supplied, gently nudging his arm. "You crashed into my car, but didn't have your license…remember?"

He shook his head, embarrassed. "Oh, right. Wait—I thought I brought you coffee?"

Jess leaned slightly closer, letting her shoulder brush his. "No, sweetie. That's when you proposed to me." Her tone was teasing, but her pulse thumped in response to the way he was looking at her—so intent, so unguarded.

He rubbed the back of his neck, a faint smile tugging at his lips. "Yeah…of course. You saved me. And then I—" He paused, gaze flicking down to her lips before snapping back to her eyes. "Anyway, that's how we met. Simple, right?"

"Simple," she echoed, but the day seemed to be anything but. From the look of things, she wasn't the only one struggling with focus today.

Jess knew she was just playing her part for the wedding, but still, she felt a strange, fluttering warm sensation at how natural it all seemed. She felt at home here, as if she truly belonged, and maybe for this one weekend, she did. She had never felt like such a rock star—the center of attention as Nolan's mystery girl. Everyone laughed at her jokes and showered her with warm, sunny smiles.

She let herself sink into it, trying to ignore the

soft, hollow ache in her belly that said this closeness was just temporary. She was borrowing a version of life she couldn't have and knowing it would end all too soon left a lump in her throat. It would be nice to have this life. Nolan as her attentive lover, and a family that was steady, familiar, and full of care for her.

Abigail appeared at Nolan's shoulder. "Almost time for the toast, son."

He nodded, and they walked toward the tent where the wedding dinner would be served. Nolan stopped by the bar to get Jess a glass of wine for the toast, then grazed her cheek with a kiss before he left.

Jess joined Nolan's family at their table. Connor was red-faced with happiness and Lauren made an absolutely gorgeous bride. Her three boys were everywhere—running all over the grassy lawn, playing hide-and-seek under the table linens. Good thing this was an outdoor wedding, Jess thought.

Caterers buzzed about like bees, adding finishing touches to a buffet of grilled vegetables and chicken, fresh breads, local cheeses, and bowls of sun-warmed stone fruit that tasted like summer. It was a picture-perfect wedding.

When everyone was seated, Nolan walked to the podium and cleared his throat. Jess took a seat next to Nolan's parents and sipped her wine. She could see how nervous he was. Nolan hated public speaking.

Nolan tapped the microphone twice. He shared a quick memory of his and Connor's childhood growing up on the vineyard, then focused on the couple. "I never imagined Connor as a family man, so when he told me he was engaged to Lauren and would be an insta-dad to her extremely energetic boys..."

As if on cue, Lauren's youngest son swooped in front of the podium, pretending to be an airplane, and zoomed off. Everyone laughed.

Nolan looked up in surprise, unaware of the recent flyby, "I just couldn't imagine how that was going to work. My brother's been a bachelor and professional athlete for years—what does he know about being a husband or father?"

Jess leaned forward slightly in her chair, pretending to adjust her dress, but her eyes were locked on Nolan. His voice was steady, but there was a raw edge beneath the polish, a trace of the man she had glimpsed in private—the man who had let her see the parts of him he hid from the world. Every time he glanced at her, she felt the familiar heat of awareness, that tight pull in her chest that made her breath catch.

"But then I saw them together," Nolan continued, sweeping his gaze over the crowd, "and now I understand. When you fall for someone—like really fall for them—well, everything changes. Your heart says, 'I don't care how complicated this gets, I want you.'"

Jess's pulse quickened. He shifted slightly, and she felt a ripple of recognition when his eyes found hers. "Love is messy. It's challenging. It will push you in ways you never expected. But it's also the thing that teaches you who you can become—how much you can grow, and how brave you can really be." He smiled faintly, tipping his head toward her. It was subtle; no one probably noticed but her. But she knew that much of this speech was meant for her.

The realization hit her all at once—bright and almost dizzying—that this wasn't just her making meaning out of nothing. Delight flared deep in her heart, warm and disbelieving, because for the first time she understood that the feelings she'd been trying so hard to hide were quietly, impossibly, being met on the other side.

"Love is a leap of faith, that much I know for sure. But if we are very lucky, the person we leap with is willing to put their trust in you too. And together, you become both the adventure and the parachute."

Applause erupted around them, but Jess barely noticed. Her gaze stayed on him, and for a moment, it was just the two of them, caught in the quiet acknowledgment that something very messy was unfolding between them.

Nolan flashed her a sweet, private smile, then turned back to the wedding table. "To Lauren and Connor," he said, raising his champagne flute high.

Jess raised her glass high. And when she tasted that sweet wine, a small, daring hope flared in her chest—maybe the future could bring her happiness that would last longer than just a weekend.

Nolan slid back into his seat at the Stone family table like he hadn't just emotionally wrecked her in front of two hundred wedding guests. As if he hadn't stood up there in the shirt and tie she had hand-selected for him and, in a devastatingly calm tone, talked about choosing love even when it terrified you. About risking what you had for something that could be good, just because the alternative was a lifetime of wondering *what if.*

And he had been looking straight at her for most of it.

Jess kept her gaze on her wineglass as he sat down beside her, the soft fabric of his pants brushing her bare knee.

"Very nice toast," she said, keeping her gaze averted. She just didn't trust herself to look into his dark brown eyes at that moment. Too many emotions swirling in her heart—too many possibilities in her head.

His knee bumped hers under the table. Not hard, but it didn't feel accidental either. A flare of heat bloomed along her skin, fast and traitorous. She shifted her leg an inch away.

His leg followed. Her stomach tightened. Was this what they were doing now?

A server squeezed between their chairs, balancing a tray of wineglasses. Nolan's hand came up automatically, settling at the hollow of Jess's back to steady her chair. His thumb lingered for a half second, protective and intimate.

Jess forgot how to breathe.

"Sorry," he murmured near her ear. His breath skimmed her skin. Her pulse jumped hard enough to make her dizzy.

"You're forgiven," she said, but what she meant was *no, you're not*. Nolan was not a man who made mistakes. Everything he did was considered, calculated, and strategized before execution.

Nolan Stone was making his move.

Across the table, Nolan's mother watched them with soft, speculative eyes. Jess felt heat crawl up her neck.

Get a grip. You are at a wedding. You are not fifteen. You are a doctor with a mortgage and unresolved trauma.

Nolan leaned closer, ostensibly to look at the slideshow starting up on the big screen.

"Check out Connor's college haircut," he murmured. "I feel like that was a cry for help."

She snorted despite herself. "Definitely in need of a family intervention."

His mouth curved, small and tender. Not his public smile. The one she'd been seeing more and more of lately. The unguarded one reserved just for her. The one that made her toes curl in her shoes.

Servers appeared at the table, delivering the first course of the wedding dinner in shallow white bowls: a chilled heirloom tomato gazpacho scattered with tiny mozzarella pearls and cracked black pepper.

Nolan leaned into her space to make room for the server, his shoulder brushing hers. But when the server moved on, Nolan's steady pressure remained. She did not pull away.

Jess became acutely aware of every point of contact between them—the warmth of his arm against hers, the press of his knee, the faint citrus-and-clean scent of his cologne.

Keeping her attraction under control was getting so much harder. So was contemplating where she would be in twenty-four hours: back in San Francisco, with no need to pose as anything other than Nolan's colleague and friend.

Afternoon became evening. The servers cleared dishes from the wedding dinner and served slices of the gorgeous wedding cake. A band took their place on a temporary stage and set up for the evening. Chairs scraped back, ties were loosened, and the energy of the evening shifted toward a night of dancing.

Their first set was something loud and high-energy with a pounding bassline that rattled the champagne flutes. Guests cheered and surged toward the dance floor.

Jess grimaced. "Oh no. Not *that* playlist."

Nolan huffed a quiet laugh. "So, I guess I shouldn't ask you for a dance?"

She rolled her eyes. "Not to whatever this is."

He leaned in, close enough that only she could hear him over the music. "Want to stick around for a better song," he asked softly, "or get a tour of the vineyard?"

Jess glanced at the dance floor. Her pulse was already racing just sitting next to him. But staying here kept them in the lanes they had staked out long ago.

She looked back at Nolan. At his steady eyes, and the quiet intensity she found there.

"Tour," she said.

His jaw tightened. Just a fraction. "Good choice," he murmured.

He stood first, offering her his hand. Jess took it. They slipped away from the family table, weaving past laughing guests and thudding music, stepping into the cooler, quieter air at the edge of the vineyard. As soon as they left the lights behind, the tension between them sharpened into something that felt coiled and electric.

Jess's heart was already in her throat. Whatever was about to happen, it had started the second he sat down beside her.

They walked in silence at first, which felt soothing after the long day of photographs, toasts, and endless chitchat. Here with Nolan, the quiet pressed her from all sides, thick with possibility.

The gravel path crunched softly under their shoes as they walked. The air carried the faint, sweet smell of grapes and night-blooming flowers. They drifted deeper into the property until the gravel path narrowed, giving way to a quieter lane bordered by low stone walls and climbing jasmine. The music from the reception faded into a distant, muffled thrum, like a memory instead of a sound.

When they rounded a bend in the path, a charming small cottage came into view. It was set back from the main vineyard road, cute as a button. White clapboard. Dark green shutters. A low sloping roofline that made it look like something out of a watercolor painting.

"What's this?" she asked.

"The old caretaker's cottage," he said. "It's been empty for over a year. The caretaker retired last summer, so we're renovating it now. Once it's finished, we'll start looking for a replacement."

Jess took a few steps closer, drawn in despite herself. Through the front window, she could see bare walls, drop cloths, a ladder propped against one corner. The place looked half finished and oddly intimate in the low glow of the porch light.

Nolan glanced at her, then back at the cottage. "You want to see what they've done so far?" he asked.

Her pulse spiked hard enough to make her dizzy. She absolutely knew what walking into that cottage would mean.

Her voice came out thin. "That would be a bad idea, wouldn't it?"

His expression was knowing. "The worst."

The silence stretched, fragile and charged, and felt like the last electric minutes before a storm breaks.

Nolan took a deep breath. "This weekend changed something for me."

Jess shifted her weight, the gravel crunching again, grounding her. Resistance to anything that could hurt her heart again still flared strong.

"You know weddings make people sentimental, Nolan. There's champagne. String lights. It's a whole psychological trap."

He took a step closer. Closing the distance enough that she could feel the heat of him.

"This isn't champagne," he said quietly. "And it's not sentimentality."

Her pulse started to stutter an unsteady beat. She knew that too.

"I know this was supposed to be a weekend of make-believe. That's all I planned to sign up for, that's for sure. But the past few weeks have made it clear that something's changed. And I'm done pretending I don't want you." His hands flexed, then stilled. "It's dishonest. And exhausting."

Jess stared at him and knew there was no coming back from this. He was taking emotional honesty farther than she had ever expected him to. Than she ever believed he *could*.

He was putting words to feelings she wasn't sure she was ready to think about.

"I'm not asking for anything," he said. "I'm not trying to complicate your life. I'm not trying to turn this into some big, complicated thing."

Her chest tightened. She felt so caught between just taking a giant leap of faith with him and trusting that the parachute would be there—or returning to her life, safe but bland, in San Francisco.

"I just don't want to lie about it anymore."

There were a million reasons for her to turn around and head back to the reception. Instead, she took a breath that felt like stepping off a cliff.

"What if we just…" she started, then faltered, then forced the words out. "What if we just get this out of our system?"

Nolan went very still. "You're serious."

She nodded, even though her hands were trembling. "Just one night," she said quickly. "No promises. No future talk. No pretending this means anything more than what it is."

"Just tonight," he said. "No consequences."

"Yeah," Jess breathed. She stepped past him toward the front door. Her hand hovered over the doorknob. *Last chance to walk away, coward.*

Then she turned the knob.

The bedroom was small and simply furnished. A nightstand with a single lamp. An open suitcase of renovation tools shoved into one corner. The bed was bare, but Nolan found sheets and a quilt packed away in a closet, and they made the bed together.

He met her near the edge of the bed and searched her face like he was memorizing it.

"You okay?" he murmured.

Her chin tipped up a fraction. Inviting him to take the next step.

As soon as he kissed her, Jess knew that everything was different.

There was no pause or hesitation. No urge to crack a joke and get back to safe ground. His mouth found hers with intention, and her body answered just as decisively, before her mind could interfere.

This time, they weren't going to stop.

The realization arrived fully formed, calm and terrifying in its certainty. A simple statement of fact. Her mind fought valiantly to find a reason she should resist, but there was no foothold for doubt. Nolan's hands were firm at her waist, thumbs pressing in, anchoring her to this moment—and to him.

Suddenly the effort of resisting felt exhausting. It was time to stop running.

Her lips parted, and she felt him kiss her deep and hard. She gave up the space where she tried to hide when her fake feelings started getting far too real. The pressure of his kiss deepened, and something inside her unlocked so fast, she had to clutch fistfuls of his shirt to stay upright.

She breathed him in, getting her fill of his soap-scented skin and husky notes. She could do this now because it wasn't love. It didn't matter. She and Nolan could ride the riptide of this desire until it released them into calmer waters.

Her legs were trembling as she slid her hands under his jacket, over the firm plane of his chest, feeling the heat of him through layers of clothing. His muscles shifted beneath her palms as he pulled her closer, closing the distance.

It became a dance without either of them deciding it should. They moved together, then apart, then together again, instinctively adjusting to the other's move. His fingers threaded into her hair, tugging just enough to make her gasp. Her hands skimmed the familiar lines of his shoulders and back, learning him through touch.

They kept finding each other. Over and over again.

His hands guided her back until the bed's edge pressed into the backs of her thighs; she fully surrendered to everything she wanted from this moment—and from him.

"Jess," he murmured.

The way he said her name—low, roughened, threaded with something dangerously close to reverence—made her chest ache. He laid her back gently on the bed, making her feel precious. The coolness of the sheets startled her, until his body warmed her with his heat and weight.

He undressed her slowly and she marveled at his self-control. Each movement felt intentional. He let his eyes linger, making warmth bloom everywhere his gaze landed.

She felt seen. And so very wanted. She didn't rush him or hide or deflect with humor. She let him look. Let herself be seen.

And when he stripped for her, she watched openly, greedily. Here was Nolan Stone in her world—precise, disciplined, controlled—seeing him like this felt like discovering he was a doctor by day, secret superhero by night.

When he finally closed the distance between them completely, the sensation stole the air from her lungs.

It wasn't just physical, though her body felt ravenous after these weeks of deprivation. Something clicked between them, so that she had regained her footing after being off-kilter for so long. She gasped softly when he dipped to meet her, her fingers digging into his shoulders, her body arching to meet him without hesitation.

The pleasure was deep and immediate and overwhelming. *Divine*, she thought. To finally be with him. To stop saying no to something her body—and her heart—had wanted so much and for so long.

His strokes were measured and deep, striking

those secret pleasure zones hidden deep in her body. Even here, he was still Nolan—attentive, controlled, utterly present. He watched her closely, adjusting his movements to her breath, her moans, the way her hands tightened when he moved just right.

She watched him too. Moonlight streamed through the bedroom window, highlighting his hair so it appeared silvery blue at the tips. It softened him, so that he looked less guarded, more vulnerable.

"God, Jess," he breathed, resting his forehead briefly against hers. "I have wanted you. So much."

The truth in his voice tightened something in her chest.

Nolan Stone, the lover, was a surprise—an artist with his hips, with his hands, with the way he let sensation build instead of chasing it. He slowed his strokes, letting her catch up. Letting her feel *everything.*

And then, though she hadn't said a word, he drove them harder, deeper. Somehow knowing she was ready before she knew it herself. Sensations blurred, time froze, until a coil of pleasure built, crested, and finally broke.

When Jess shattered around him, it felt like releasing her grip on reality so she could fly. All the control she had clutched at slipped through her fingers and disappeared.

But she wasn't scared. Not with Nolan.

They stayed there afterward, breathing slowly as the world came back into focus. Nolan brushed a strand of hair away from her face, his thumb lingering against her lip. His smile was slow, satisfied, unmistakably real.

"I'm not done with you yet," he whispered.

Daammnn, she thought. Who was this sex god, and what had he done with Nolan Stone?

They rested wrapped in warmth, tucked beneath the quilt. They talked quietly about nothing and everything. Connor's wedding. A patient story. A joke.

As the wind whispered its secrets against the window, they made love again.

He rolled her to her stomach and took her slower, even deeper. Learning every inch of her body until her thoughts scattered like dust motes in a breeze. She was out of her mind with pleasure. All she could do was grab fistfuls of her sheets and moan through her orgasms, hoping she wouldn't pass out from sheer bliss.

It felt too good. *He* felt too good. And beneath the pleasure, something else stirred—something unmooring from its anchor in her chest. Everything that had grounded her since Evan left—her work, her plans, her fighting spirit—blurred at the edges. None of it felt important.

There was just Nolan.

Afterward, he tucked the quilt around her carefully and kissed her temple.

She let out a soft, shaky laugh. "I think I am very bad at getting things out of my system."

Nolan turned onto his side, propping his head on his hand, his gaze tender and unguarded. "I think I am too."

She turned her head to look at him. She was definitely falling for Nolan.

"What are we going to do?"

He didn't say a word. Just pulled her into him and wrapped his arms around her so that she felt totally sheltered and protected. She closed her eyes, pressed her face into his chest, and let herself believe this would all make sense in the morning.

CHAPTER NINE

THE NURSES' STATION was a steady hum of activity. Jess leaned against the counter reviewing a chart, the sound of keyboards clicking and monitors chiming keeping her company.

Nolan suddenly stepped into her space. She looked up in surprise. "What are you doing on my turf?" she asked.

He slid a hot cup of coffee her way. "Bringing you this. Now drink it. Before it goes cold and tragic like the last one."

Their fingers brushed as she took the cup, lingering just long enough to feel intentional.

It still startled her, sometimes, how easily *after the wedding* had turned into *after most shifts*, their supposed one-night detour quietly stretching into something neither of them had named yet. They weren't exactly a couple—at least not in any clean, public way—but they were no longer pretending it was nothing either. Just…something real, unfolding between pages and consults, without rules for what came next.

And until they officially returned the engagement ring, she was free to live in this space between being Nolan's fake fiancée and his real life… whatever.

Just then the overhead pager crackled to life. "Trauma team to the ED. Incoming pediatric MVA. Two minutes out."

Nolan looked up from his phone to catch her gaze.

"You should stick around," she teased. "Maybe you'll learn something."

He rolled his eyes but after that, it was all business. The air shifted instantly. Nolan straightened. Jess set her coffee down.

The pediatric trauma bay snapped to life as soon as the EMTs burst through the ED doors with their gurney.

"Four-year-old female, restrained passenger, high-speed MVA," the paramedic called out. "Airbags deployed. Brief loss of consciousness. Hypotensive en route."

Jess was already on the move. She snapped on gloves as she and Nolan met at the foot of the bed. The room was soon filled with nurses and ED doctors, all focused on their young patient.

"On three!" Jess called. "One, two…"

The EMTs transferred the little girl onto the bed. She was impossibly small under all those monitoring wires and oxygen tubing. Jess watched her chest, not liking the fast, shallow breaths she saw.

A nurse called out. "Heart rate one forty. Pressure eighty-five systolic."

Jess leaned in. "Hi, sweetheart. My name is Jess. You are in a hospital now, and we are going to help you. Can you hear me?"

The girl whimpered, eyelids fluttering.

Nolan joined her. "Breath sounds are diminished on the right."

"Prep for chest X-ray," Jess instructed. "FAST exam now."

The room became a busy hive of activity and sound. Scissors cut fabric, monitors beeped, voices shouted out vitals. Jess slid the ultrasound probe over the girl's abdomen, her jaw tightening when dark fluid appeared on the screen.

"Positive FAST," Nolan confirmed.

"Call pediatric surgery," Jess commanded. "Stat."

The stakes were high for this child, but not catastrophic. She had bleeding and internal injuries. Serious, for sure, but survivable.

So, Jess was disappointed when the girl's blood pressure dipped after being stable for several minutes.

"Eighty systolic!" the nurse called.

Jess frowned and pressed her fingers into the girl's abdomen. There was a rigid guarding beneath her palm. Something didn't feel right.

"Her belly's getting tighter," she said. "And she's still hypotensive despite fluids."

Dr. Campbell, an attending in the surgical/critical care unit, spoke up. "We can get a CT to localize the bleed before surgery takes over."

Jess shook her head. "She's too unstable. She should go straight to OR. Pediatric surgery can find and control whatever's wrong faster than we can image it."

Dr. Campbell disagreed. "Dr. Hayes, we don't have to rush to make a bad decision just to say we did something." His gaze scanned the room and settled on Nolan. "Stone, speak up here. Would you send this patient off to CT or straight to surgery?"

Jess could not believe this was happening. A little girl was deteriorating right in front of them, and Dr. Campbell was turning this into a competition.

But Nolan would back her up. She was certain of that. So certain that she almost gave the order to prep the girl for surgery when Nolan suddenly spoke up.

"Protocol recommends CT localization before exploratory surgery when vitals are temporarily stabilized."

Jess's jaw fell open as she shifted her gaze to Nolan. He met her gaze head-on, his expression calm and in control.

"We've seen this before," she reminded him. "Remember the Miller case? CT just delayed surgery, and that little boy crashed on the table."

Nolan's jaw tightened. He didn't respond immediately.

What was wrong here? His gaze flicked to the doorway where the attending hovered, arms crossed with a self-satisfied grin.

Jess leaned in and practically hissed, "Protocol also says we don't delay definitive care in a crashing pediatric patient."

"She's not crashing," he countered. "She's borderline. We can spare ten minutes to find the bleed."

"You're going to risk her life for ten minutes?"

"Are you?"

The attending cleared his throat. "We need a decision, Doctors."

Jess didn't break eye contact with Nolan. *You said you trusted my instincts. Why won't you back me up?*

Nolan's gaze was just as steady. "We have time."

Jess's chest hollowed out. She couldn't believe he wasn't on her side.

The attending waited. "Jess?"

Jess asked for an update on the girl's vitals. She was not in a full-blown crisis, but she wasn't well either. Still borderline, as she had been since she came into the ED.

"Order the CT."

The charge nurse snatched up the wall phone and punched in the CT extension from memory, her other hand already scribbling on the trauma flow sheet.

"CT, this is ED," she said. "I've got a stat belly

coming your way. Trauma bay two. Pediatric. Hemodynamically tenuous."

After a flurry of activity to prep the girl for transport, the gurney lurched forward. Jess walked alongside the head of the bed, one palm braced against the mattress rail, eyes locked on the child's face.

"Pressure?" she asked.

"Eighty-six systolic and holding," the nurse said.

Not great. Not catastrophic.

They hit the threshold between the trauma bay and hallway. Double doors swung open and then her team turned the corner to radiology.

Jess peeled off her gloves with clumsy fingers and headed back to the ED. The trauma bay was empty, the bed was stripped.

The adrenaline drained out of her all at once, leaving her hollow and trembling. Her hands shook as she balled the gloves and dropped them into the biohazard bin. Her shoulders sagged as the weight of the last hour settled into her bones.

Nolan was still there, standing at the computer station, his back half turned to her, already charting. His fingers moved with precise, relentless efficiency.

Something small and sharp twisted in her chest. So this was how he wanted to play it? Like nothing had happened?

Her throat tightened. She squared her shoulders, forcing her breathing to steady.

Professional. Fine. She could do professional.

"Post-op labs are ordered," she said, keeping her tone neutral, clinical. "ICU bed's assigned."

"Good," he said. He broke away from his work and turned to face her, his expression maddeningly placid. "You okay?"

Her fingers curled into her palms. She stared at him, at the lines of his face that were starting to become familiar to her now. Or so she had thought.

Fluorescent lights buzzed overhead. Somewhere in the ED, a code alarm wailed and cut off again.

"Jess?"

Her pulse thudded against her ribs. Her hands were shaking again, damn it, the adrenaline crash making her feel raw and exposed.

"I thought you trusted me," she said quietly. "I thought you had my back. Or is that only when we're alone?"

He blinked, genuinely startled. "That's not fair."

Something hot and bitter flared in her chest. "It's exactly fair."

He shook his head, armoring up. "I followed protocol."

"I know." The words made her throat feel raw. Nolan's need to follow protocol at all costs was the problem.

"Then why are you acting like I betrayed you?" he demanded.

Her breath caught. "Because you did," she said. "You told me after that choking case that my judgment saved that little girl from an unnecessary tracheotomy."

The trauma bay felt too small. Too tight.

He dragged a hand through his hair, the motion sharp and restless. "Sure, Jess. But that was a different case. This patient needed surgery, and I think taking the time to locate the bleed was important for reducing her risk."

Her laugh was dry and brittle. "Was it patient risk you were worried about, Nolan? Or risks to your career? You don't get to put me on a shelf, and only pull me out when it's convenient." Her voice was trembling now despite her desperate effort to stay calm. "You don't get to trust me when it's easy and pull back when it costs you something."

"I didn't pull back," he insisted. "I made a responsible call."

"That's your armor talking."

His jaw tightened, the muscle jumping. "You're asking me to gamble with a child's life."

Her chest felt tight and constricted. "I was asking you to value me more than your reputation."

He stared at her. He didn't answer.

Something inside her sagged. He still didn't understand. He would never understand. She'd spent *decades* of her life making herself small for her father and then Evan so that loving her never inconvenienced them. Her needs always came second.

"Nolan, I can't do this," she said quietly. Her voice sounded far away. "You are who you are.

You'll always trust rules and protocols more than you trust me."

"That's not true."

"You just proved it is." The words left a bitter aftertaste as soon as she said them.

She took a step back, the distance between them suddenly unbearable and necessary all at once. She waited for him to say something else. To argue or reach for her. To promise her something—anything—even if he couldn't yet understand how to give it.

But he didn't. He just watched her with an impenetrable expression. It was hopeless. *They* were hopeless. As a fake couple, they had some fun. But they were way too different to ever work in real life.

"Bye, Nolan."

She left the trauma bay and headed for the locker room, forbidding herself from looking back.

The first thing Jess noticed was how quiet her apartment felt without Nolan in it.

Not physically—he hadn't been there often enough for his absence to leave a literal imprint—but emotionally. The air felt different, like something essential had been removed and the room hadn't adjusted yet. The silence felt so wide and empty, and she caught herself listening for footsteps that weren't coming.

She dropped her keys into the ceramic bowl by

the door and stood there longer than she meant to, staring at nothing.

You did the right thing.

She had told herself that nearly every hour since leaving Nolan alone in the trauma bay. It didn't make the ache in her chest any better.

Thank goodness for work. It was practically the only thing that got her through the first few days after their fight. Jess moved through her shifts like a robot, letting muscle memory take over. Her hands were steady. Her voice was calm. Her instincts were sharp. She stabilized patients before sending them off to the ICU, to surgery, to a pediatric ward to recover. Everyone trusted her judgment. Nurses trusted her without question.

Yet she had never felt like more of an imposter in her life.

Every time she reached for her phone between cases, she stopped to warn herself. *Don't expect a text from him.* At first, she tried to believe she didn't *want* to hear from him. But every time she saw a tall man in navy scrubs around the hospital, she knew she was a liar.

There were no texts.

He was somewhere in this hospital with her. Two professionals existing in the same space, like two planets whose orbits no longer intersected.

It made her so aware of all the empty universes between them.

The third night after the fight, she poured herself a glass of wine and sat cross-legged on the couch. She intended to lose herself in a movie, but the images just rolled one after another without ever registering in her mind.

Her mind was too busy torturing her with memories she hadn't invited.

How he had looked at her at his brother's rehearsal dinner, quiet and reverent, like he couldn't believe she was there.

The way he'd curled his arm around her in his sleep, unconsciously giving her a safe place to rest.

The way he'd kissed her in the consult room, deliberate and unguarded, finally giving her a glimpse at the vulnerable man who hid behind his mask.

She pressed her palm against her sternum. It did nothing to ease the cold weight that had settled in her gut.

You ended it because you had to be right.

I was right! That little girl...

Ugh. Enough.

There had been more than one option in the ED that day. She hadn't thought so initially, when the girl first came in, but they had been able to stabilize her to borderline status. Jess could have insisted on sending the girl to surgery, and no one would have questioned her judgment.

But taking the time to send her for imaging

wasn't wrong either. It took extra time and brought some extra risk. But it also gave the surgeons more precise information before they operated.

She had held her ground not because the patient needed that from her.

She had held her ground because Nolan's refusal to side with her felt like abandonment. He was, she had decided at that moment, just another man who would let her down when she needed him most.

My god, was I testing him?

She hoped not. She hoped she would never do anything to jeopardize a patient for her own ego or emotional issues. But the fact was, she and Nolan should be able to disagree on protocols, treatments, or even where to eat dinner without it feeling like she was trapped in a life-and-death struggle for survival.

She thought she was over Evan, and she was. But she wasn't over the patterns that triggered her profound defenses. The fear that she would fall for someone who would give her scraps and call it love. Who would care for her just enough to keep her attached, then disappear when she truly needed him.

Nolan wasn't Evan—but she was making him pay the price anyway.

The door clicked shut behind Nolan with a hollow finality that echoed through the space.

Nothing disturbed the silence. No one sang in the kitchen while making dinner. No rhythmic clatter of dishes in the kitchen.

His home was perfectly clean, meticulously organized, utterly silent. And empty.

His chest tightened. This should have felt normal. This had been his life for years—controlled, orderly, solitary.

Instead, it felt like something vital had been removed while he wasn't looking.

He stood just inside the door, keys still in his hand, listening to nothing.

His grip tightened. He set the keys on the entry table with clinical precision. Loosened his tie. Shrugged out of his suit jacket and draped it over the back of a chair. Lined his shoes up exactly beside the door.

He didn't remember deciding to do any of it. He was busy replaying her words in his head.

I'm asking you to value me more than you value your reputation.

He dragged a hand over his face and exhaled hard. That had not been fair.

He had followed protocol so he could make the safest call. That's what he had spent his life training to do.

He had been right. He was sure of it.

So why did it feel like he'd just lost something he might never get back?

* * *

At work the next morning, the praise came fast and casual.

"Good call with the CT," Dr. Campbell said, clapping him on the shoulder. "Textbook management."

Nolan forced a smile. Textbook.

The word landed like an insult. His jaw tightened and he turned back to his computer and found the little girl's chart.

She was doing well in the PICU. Her surgery had gone well with no complications. By every metric that mattered on paper, her treatment had been a success.

So, he had been right. There *had* been enough time for the CT scan. But instead of feeling vindicated, his chest just ached.

After no calls or texts from Jess, he invented some reason to visit the ED. But apparently she had just left.

That night, after his shift at the hospital, he went home and poured himself a drink he didn't want. He swirled the amber liquid until the ice cube clinked against his glass.

He carried it into the living room and sat on the edge of the couch. The blank television screen reflected his silhouette back at him.

He stared at it. The moment replayed itself again.

The ultrasound results. The little girl's vitals.

The brief window they had to stabilize her before surgery.

We don't delay care in crashing pediatric cases, she had told him.

She's borderline—we have time, he had told her.

Two defensible options. They had both been right.

He had chosen the safer one.

His chest tightened as Jess's face rose unbidden in his mind. Quiet, wounded, and resolute.

Trusting him to see what she saw. Or, if he couldn't, to trust her judgment.

He closed his eyes. This wasn't about medicine. He knew that now.

Nolan finished his drink as he scrolled through old pictures on his phone.

One image hit him without warning. He was nine years old in this one. Way too small for his pads. Too slow for those football drills too.

He remembered that day, and how Connor had streaked down the field, effortless, magnetic.

How his father's jaw would clench when Nolan missed another tackle.

"You're just not built for this," his father had said once, not unkindly. "Find something else."

Shame had curled low in his gut. But he had listened. Through books and grades and scores and metrics, he had found the one arena where *he* could compete…and win.

Being strong or fast did not matter in the world of medicine. Medicine was perfect for him.

In medicine, there were protocols. Algorithms. Ways to quantify risk and minimize it.

In medicine, you didn't have to guess how much someone mattered. You followed the steps and the outcome took care of itself.

That's how *he* stayed safe. That's how he earned his father's love and approval. Achievement, success, safety.

Sleep eluded him that night. All he could think about was Jess. Her hand on the child's abdomen. The set of her jaw. And how she had looked at him.

Not angry. Searching, trusting—and then so, so hurt.

He *had* trusted her gut before. So why not this time?

He squeezed his eyes shut, not wanting to see the truth. Because someone from administration was watching. An authority figure. He had known the case would be reviewed. That whatever he supported *might* be called into question.

Jess made her decision from the gut, based on all the patients she had treated in the ED before that little girl.

Nolan made his decision from the head, based on all the protocols and rules he trusted to keep him safe.

His hands balled into loose fists. This time, following the textbook had cost him Jess. He had lost her because he was afraid.

He leaned forward on the couch, pressing his forearms against his thighs. Bowed his head. He had told himself he was protecting the patient. But that wasn't the full truth.

He had been protecting himself just as much. From blame and regret and vulnerability.

From choosing her over all the things that he believed kept him safe from ever hearing *you're not good enough.*

Jess hadn't asked him to gamble with a child's life. She had asked him to gamble with his heart.

He'd refused and he had failed her.

CHAPTER TEN

JESS STOOD AT her bathroom mirror, her toothbrush hovering near her face, loaded with minty, cavity-fighting protection.

"I'm not afraid of dating a colleague," she said out loud. She had been reading a lot lately. How to heal childhood wounds. How to face her fears by repeating mantras until they felt true could help, the books said.

"I'm not afraid of dating a colleague," she said again. It still didn't feel true.

"I'm afraid of loving someone who freezes when I need them."

The words echoed back at her, confirming what she already knew.

"I am afraid of loving Nolan," she whispered. That statement was straight-punch-to-the-gut true. She *was* terrified of falling for Nolan. Because she wasn't sure she could survive if Nolan could only love and believe in her so long as it was easy and convenient.

And yet…

Her mind threw up all sorts of counterevidence. How he brought her coffee at the hospital without being asked. All the effort she knew he must have invested to find that album for her. And how readily he shared credit for their patient wins, like the teenager with the subtle signs of meningitis.

In ways large and small, Nolan had made himself vulnerable for her. He had tried to close the distance between them in a thousand small ways that weren't grand or showy, but felt like devotion. Just like her patient, James, before he died. Not telling his wife he loved her. *Showing* her, by tending to the small, mundane details that made up the sum of their life together.

Nolan had been trying all along. She just didn't always have the eyes, or heart, to see it.

She went for a long walk along the waterfront that evening, hands stuffed in her sweatshirt, the air sharp on her cheeks.

People passed her in pairs and families, and laughing clusters of friends.

It made her heart ache being alone out there. She wondered what Nolan was doing. She hated that she still cared.

You made the right choice.

Those mantra people were wrong. She had been repeating that mantra for days and it still didn't feel true.

The truth was, walking away hadn't solved a

thing, nor had it protected her. It had just amplified her loss.

She stopped at a bench and sat down, staring out at the choppy water.

What if she had misread him that day? What if his hesitation hadn't been a lack of faith in her. What if it had been fear?

It still didn't make it okay. But it did make him human.

Suddenly, the story she had tried to believe—that Nolan would always choose safety over her—felt less solid than it did when she walked away from Nolan in the trauma bay.

People didn't grow by being perfect. They didn't grow by thinking they were right all the time either.

They grew by learning and doing better the next time.

Sometimes a good dose of healing was needed too.

She pulled out her phone and scrolled to his name. She almost texted him but made herself stop. She wasn't ready to reach out yet. She was certain of that.

But an hour later, she was standing in her kitchen, her forehead pressed against the freezer door as she realized she was done. Done with fighting and mantras and trying to believe that letting go of Nolan was going to be easy.

Her emotional reserves were drained.

"I don't want to be without him," she whispered. The admission felt like a surrender. To love and risk and to admitting that trying to protect herself hadn't actually made her safe.

It had just made her lonely.

The absurd idea came to him at three in the morning.

Nolan was sitting at his dining table, laptop open, untouched glass of water beside him. He had been trying to read his emails, but the letters and symbols just refused to make sense.

He pulled a pad of paper from his laptop bag. Across the top he had written *Jess Hayes—Known Data Points.* Below that, a list.

- Is good at connecting with patients and people
- Is bad at picking scrubs that don't blind co-workers
- Loves animals, travel, food adventures
- Has good taste in music

In hindsight, his idea to study Jess and find a way to earn her trust had been…so him. Reducing her to a series of variables he thought he could master.

A blank document glowed on the screen. He typed her name again. *Jess.* The cursor blinked at him relentlessly. It felt like a taunt. *How are you going to make things right, big guy?*

A low throb filled his head. He didn't know how to do this without structure. How to speak from his heart without preparation. Or be brave without a framework.

But he *did* know how to build an argument. And lay out evidence. Make his case.

A soft, incredulous laugh slipped out of him. He wasn't really going to try to win her heart *this* way, was he?

Shaking his head, he opened the PowerPoint program on his laptop. What an insane and ridiculous idea. *So Nolan*, he could hear her say.

But maybe it would work. It was all he had, really. Sitting across from her and pouring his heart out would never work. The words would just get all jumbled up in his mind.

His fingers began to move.

Slide One: What I'm Good At

He paused to think, then let his fingers fly across the keyboard.

Slide Two: What I'm Bad At

This one was fast and easy.

Slide Three: The Pattern

This one took a little longer, because it hurt to be honest.

He finished the rest of the slides over the next hour, each one a sort of confession and a catharsis at the same time. By the time he was done, he'd seen his mistake.

It wasn't Jess's data points he needed to understand. It was his own.

He closed the laptop. He felt exhausted and drained and free.

His heart was pounding. Not because he thought this would win her back. Because for the first time in his life, he was stepping into the unknown.

She didn't decide to take him back. But she did decide to listen.

If he came back—if he still wanted her—if he wanted to try to change…then she would listen.

They had built something over the past few weeks of pretending to be two people healthy enough to fall in love and want to get married. That had to count for something, didn't it? Maybe they had experienced just enough fake trust, fake vulnerability and fake love to manage it in real life.

Maybe they had a shot.

That night, she cleaned her apartment as if she were preparing for company. She lined up her shoes, washed her wineglass, and finally took a shower. This is what you do, the books said, when you're ready to heal and have the life you want. Let go of the old, prepare for the new.

She folded the blanket on the couch and set the record player nearby.

She felt a little ridiculous. But still, she left a lamp on by the door.

The next day, he didn't rehearse or refine what he was going to do. He left the typos and the awkward phrasing.

He left the raw truth exactly as it was. He stood outside Jess's apartment building, laptop bag slung over his shoulder like a life preserver.

Are you home? I can pick up the ring today if you like.

His heart hammered in his throat as he waited for her response. He wasn't going to expect a thing from her. He just wanted to be honest.

That's fine. I'm home.

He drew in a breath, then climbed the three flights of stairs to her apartment. A new dwarf lemon tree in a blue ceramic pot was set by her door. It still had the tag dangling from a branch. A cheer-up project left abandoned for now.

A knot twisted tight in his abdomen as he raised his hand to knock.

CHAPTER ELEVEN

THE KNOCK ON Jess's door came at 7:12 p.m.

She knew the time because she'd been staring at the clock for the last ten minutes, wondering what would happen when he came to pick up the ring.

Her heart leaped anyway.

She crossed the living room slowly, palms damp, pulse hammering in her ears. Through the peephole, she saw a familiar shock of dark hair, a navy jacket she recognized, the laptop bag slung awkwardly over one shoulder.

Her stomach dropped like an elevator in freefall.

She opened the door. "Nolan," she said, the word soft and startled, as if he'd materialized out of the very hope she'd been trying not to indulge.

"Hi," he said.

He looked…different.

Not physically—he was still tall, composed, maddeningly handsome in that restrained, precise way—but something in his posture was different. His shoulders weren't squared into armor. His jaw wasn't tight with control.

He looked like a man who had come without an agenda or certainty of what would happen next.

"Is this a good time?"

She stepped aside. "Come in."

He blinked, then nodded and entered her apartment. She closed the door behind him, the click echoing too loudly in the suddenly charged silence.

They stood there, six feet apart, like strangers instead of two people who knew the landscape of each other's bodies.

"I'll get the ring," she said, trying to sound normal.

"Actually," he began.

Despite herself, Jess smiled. How many times had she teased The Professor for starting sentences with *actually*?

He indicated the laptop bag he had slung on his shoulder. "I have something to show you. A PowerPoint presentation."

Well, that made sense. What does one do after a breakup other than make a presentation?

She shook her head. "Okay."

He held up his hand, grimacing slightly. "I realize how insane that sounds. But it made sense in my head at three o'clock this morning."

Against her will, a laugh bubbled out of her. It was small and breathless and more emotional than amused.

"You broke my heart," she said, half disbelieving. "And now you're here with...slides."

"Jess," he said quietly. "I'm terrible at romance. But an absolute rock star with PowerPoint."

She crossed her arms. "Humor won't work here, Nolan."

He nodded. "Fair."

There was a beat of silence.

"I'm not here to argue," he said. "I'm not here to defend myself. I'm here to tell you what I should have told you before."

Her heart thudded painfully.

"Okay," she said. "I'll listen." That was what she had promised herself she owed him—and herself.

He set the laptop bag down on her coffee table and opened it. His hands shook just enough for her to notice.

He swallowed, then started. "I followed protocol," he said quietly. "And I told myself that made me right."

She stayed silent.

"I wasn't wrong medically," he continued. "But I was wrong about what that moment meant."

He opened the laptop.

The first slide filled the screen.

What I'm Good At
Protocol
Risk management
Predictability
Control

* * *

Jess's breath hitched.

He looked at her. "This is the part where you're allowed to laugh."

She didn't.

"I've built my entire life around these things," he said. "Because they kept me safe. Because they kept me valuable."

He clicked to the next slide.

What I'm Bad At
Vulnerability
Uncertainty
Saying what I feel without a plan

Her throat tightened.

"You already know about football," he said. "About my father. About Connor."

She nodded.

"What you don't know," he continued, voice low and steady, "is that I am scared to death of failure. I avoid it at all costs, deny it when it happens, and do everything I can to be a winner. Because for me, failure isn't a learning experience. It's a one-way ticket to losing love and respect."

He clicked again.

The Pattern
Football → failure → shame

Academics → success → safety
Medicine → control → worthiness

Jess sank onto the edge of her couch without realizing she'd moved.

"I didn't become a doctor because I wanted to save lives," he said softly. "Not at first. I became a doctor because it was the first thing I was unambiguously good at. Because it was the first place I felt…enough."

Her chest ached for him.

He clicked again.

The Mistake
I didn't choose protocol because it was right
I chose it because it was safe

He turned to face her fully.

"I saw your face when I hesitated," he said. "And I knew, even before you said it, that I had just failed you."

Her eyes burned.

"You trusted me until it mattered," she whispered.

He nodded. "Yes."

The word landed heavy between them.

He clicked again.

What Jess Taught Me
Courage isn't recklessness

Trust is an action
Love requires risk

He swallowed.

"You asked me to choose you in a moment that scared me," he said. "And I didn't."

Tears blurred her vision.

"I told myself I was protecting a child," he continued. "But I was protecting myself."

Her hands clenched in her lap.

"I'm done doing that," he said quietly.

He clicked to the final slide.

You are my Adventure. Let me be your Parachute.

He closed the laptop.

"Jess, I'm never going to be the guy that organizes a flash mob proposal or sweeps you off your feet with my perfect words. I am who I am, and that's not going to change.

"But I can take risks too. And when it comes to you, I don't want to play it safe. I want to risk everything with you—and for you."

Silence was a heavy weight in the room. Jess pressed her hand to her chest.

"You broke my heart," she said hoarsely.

"I know."

"I felt so alone."

"That was wrong. I'm sorry."

"But I was wrong too. I let *my* fears convince me that if you don't back me up, then you'll fail me when I need you most."

And something inside her finally cracked open. Her breath shuddered as she finally let go of all the hurt Evan had left behind. And to some extent, her father too.

He nodded. "You have me, Jess. Whenever you need me."

She stepped closer. "Even when it's messy, and uncertain, and terrifying—you will still choose me?"

Nolan stepped closer in response. "I'll choose us—always."

Her breath hitched as her resistance collapsed in on itself.

She closed the last inch between them. "What took you so long?"

He drew her into his arms. "I had to make a PowerPoint presentation."

She laughed, a soft, breathless sound that held more relief than humor, and dropped her forehead to his chest.

For a moment she just stood there, breathing him in. He smelled so good—like salty air from the bay mixed with that clean familiar scent that was just Nolan.

Nolan wrapped his arms around her, solid and sure, his hand settling between her shoulder blades like he was anchoring her to him. His warmth seeped through her, steadying the tremor that still lived in her bones.

Nolan felt like Home.

Her throat tightened. She tilted her head up. Found his eyes already on her, dark and intent and unguarded in a way she had never seen before.

He lowered his mouth to hers. And kissed her like a man who knew exactly what he wanted and wasn't afraid to claim it.

The world narrowed to the feel of his mouth, the gentle pressure of his hands, the quiet certainty in the way he held her. Her hands slid up his chest, fingers curling into the fabric of his jacket. She was claiming him too.

Old disappointments and fears loosened their grip. He was chasing them away as he deepened the kiss, keeping it slow and deliberate.

Steady and certain. Just like Nolan. Just like she liked it.

She made a soft sound she didn't recognize, something between a sob and a laugh, and he kissed her harder, like he felt it too. Like he understood exactly what he was undoing inside her.

When he finally drew back, they were both breathing hard.

Her eyes stung. "This is new," she whispered.

"Yes," he said, his thumb brushing her cheek, reverent. "It is."

They were building something new in this moment. Not a story to please a parent or escape an uncomfortable event. Something real and true that was just for them.

And for the first time in a long time, Jess knew it could last.

EPILOGUE

One Year Later

THE STONE FAMILY VINEYARD glowed in the late afternoon sun, rows of grapevines stretching out in soft green symmetry, their leaves whispering in the breeze. A half-assembled arch stood near the edge of the property, waiting for flowers and fabric and whatever final touches Jess hadn't yet decided on.

She stood in the middle of it all with a clipboard tucked under her arm, barefoot in the grass, a ridiculous smile she couldn't seem to shake from her face.

"You know you don't have to supervise every chair," Nolan said dryly from behind her.

She turned, hands on her hips. "I absolutely do. These are the ceremony chairs. They have to face the vineyard, not the barn."

He stepped closer, slipping his arms around her waist from behind and resting his chin on her shoulder. "You say that like there's a wrong direction to face perfection."

She laughed, leaning back into him. "Dr. Stone, if I didn't know better, I'd swear you're becoming a romantic."

He kissed the side of her neck anyway. "That's on you, buttercup."

Across the lawn, her father was arguing gently with Connor about irrigation schedules. The sight of him—sun-hatted, sleeves rolled up, clipboard in hand, looking purposeful and…content—still made Jess's chest tighten in the best way.

A year ago, she never would have imagined this life.

Her father had moved onto the property shortly after leaving rehab, into the small caretaker's cottage near the south fields. What had started as a temporary arrangement had turned into something permanent when he'd taken over day-to-day vineyard management for the Stones, putting his decades of farming experience to good use.

He had a routine now. A purpose. People who needed him.

And for the first time in her adult life, Jess didn't feel like she had made a mistake when she moved him to San Francisco.

"Earth to fiancée," Nolan murmured.

She smiled. "I was just thinking about my dad."

He followed her gaze. "He's in his element."

"I know," she said softly. "It makes me…ridiculously happy."

Nolan's arms tightened around her. "Good. Because I don't think my parents will ever give him up."

She tilted her head to look at him. "Is he part of my dowry, then?" she teased.

"Yep. Him and a lifetime supply of corn chips," he said solemnly.

They were interrupted by Abigail waving a measuring tape in the air. "Jess! Do you want the arch two feet to the left or three?"

Jess sighed theatrically. "So many decisions in one summer wedding."

Nolan took the clipboard from her hands. "I've got this," he said, already flipping to the schedule. "You go breathe for a minute."

She studied him. The man who once needed a PowerPoint to confess his feelings now coordinated floral deliveries and linen colors like it was the most natural thing in the world.

"You're very bossy for a guy whose best game was a coffee proposal."

He shrugged. "Turns out my best girl has given me better game."

She kissed him—quick, easy, full of the quiet certainty that still startled her sometimes.

"What are you thinking about?" she asked.

He glanced at her, eyes warm. "How strange it is that my life finally feels…unplanned. And better for it."

She laced her fingers through his. "Messy love?"

He smiled. "Messy love."

They stood there together as the lights flickered on overhead, the vineyard glowing around them, the future stretching out in all its complicated, beautiful uncertainty.

And for the first time in her life, Jess didn't just believe in happy endings.

She was living inside one.

* * * * *

If you enjoyed this story, check out these other great reads from Kate MacGuire

Bump in Their Italian Fling
City Doc for the Single Mum
Resisting the Off-Limits Paediatrician

All available now!